The Amish

Book Cellar

A WILLOW SPRINGS
AMISH MYSTERY ROMANCE

Book 1

Tracy Fredrychowski

ISBN: 979-8-9906105-0-7 (paperback)

ISBN: 979-8-9879040-7-7 (digital)

All Bible verses are taken from King James Version (KJV)

Published in South Carolina by The Tracer Group, LLC

https://tracyfredrychowski.com

i

Tracy Fredrychowski

"I dedicate this book to my dear husband, Craig—the one who lifts me up when I'm down, provides a voice of reason when my thoughts scatter, and continuously inspires me to be the best version of myself."

By Tracy Fredrychowski

AMISH OF LAWRENCE COUNTY SERIES

Secrets of Willow Springs – Book 1
Secrets of Willow Springs – Book 2
Secrets of Willow Springs – Book 3

APPLE BLOSSOM INN SERIES

Love Blooms at the Apple Blossom Inn
An Amish Christmas at the Apple Blossom Inn

NOVELLAS

The Amish Women of Lawrence County
An Amish Gift Worth Waiting For
The Orphan's Amish Christmas

THE AMISH WOMEN OF LAWRENCE COUNTY

Emma's Amish Faith Tested – Book 1
Rebecca's Amish Heart Restored – Book 2
Anna's Amish Fears Revealed – Book 3
Barbara's Amish Truth Exposed – Book 4
Allie's Amish Family Miracle – Book 5

A WILLOW SPRINGS AMISH MYSTERY ROMANCE

The Amish Book Cellar – Book 1

www.tracyfredrychowski.com

iii

Contents

A NOTE ABOUT AMISH VOCABULARY

The Amish language is called Pennsylvania Dutch and is usually spoken rather than written. The spelling of commonly used words varies from community to community throughout the United States and Canada. Even as I researched this book, some words' spelling changed within the same Amish community that inspired this story. In one case, spellings were debated between family members. Some of the terms may have slightly different spellings. Still, all came from my interactions with the Amish settlement near where I was raised in northwestern Pennsylvania.

While this book was modeled upon a small community in Lawrence County, this is a work of fiction. The names and characters are products of my imagination. They do not resemble any person, living or dead, or actual events in that community.

PROLOGUE

Death Stuns Prominent Family

by Jonas Butler – The Hemlock Star

Well-known Amish businessman Wally Troyer, the owner of the Book Cellar, died unexpectedly early morning, Friday, June 16. Mr. Troyer was an upstanding citizen of the Amish business community, and the local Willow Springs Police Department is investigating his untimely death.

Carpenter, Aaron Shetler, found the store's window broken on the morning of the sixteenth, leading to the discovery of Mr. Troyer's body. No suspect has been charged, and the incident is under investigation.

Mr. Troyer's estranged daughter, Lydia,

is slated to take over the store until a new owner can be established. Willow Springs's most admired meeting spot is due to resume regular hours on Monday, June 26.

CHAPTER 1
Summer - Pittsburgh, Pennsylvania

L ydia Troyer had been holding on to the dream of clinching Pittsburgh's top podcast host award for the past three years. When the wonderful news finally arrived that she had won, the thought of shopping for an outfit for the black-tie event became a laborious chore. Were it not for the support of her closest friend and confidant, Samantha Harper (affectionally known as Sami), Lydia might have been scrambling to make just anything do.

Both women had long put their roots behind them to embrace all Pittsburgh offered. Dubbed the "Simple Girls" by their fellow employees at Markle Media, they were often teased about their Christian upbringing in the liberal work environment.

Born and raised in the deep South, Sami still carried the scars of being the only daughter of a very conservative Southern preacher. On the other hand, Lydia was raised an hour north of

Pittsburgh in Willow Springs, an Old Order Amish Community. While different in many ways, their values still bore deep into their everyday lives, leaving them outcasts from the typical party scene of Pittsburgh's young professionals. While they didn't mind when they were left out, it gave them ample opportunity to gain experience in one of the city's hottest podcast publications. When their boss tasked them with finding a way to bring new authors into the firm, Lydia suggested interviewing authors about their latest releases. Still, Markle Media would need to secure some of the biggest names in the publishing industry for the podcast to be a success. Before long, some of the country's top agents were calling to secure a spot for their author clients. Now, after three grueling years, Lydia was due to be recognized at Pittsburgh's premier marketing awards event.

Sami carried a stack of dresses and led her to the fitting room. "Go on, try them on. I'm certain one of these will work."

"I don't know about this. Why can't I wear one of the outfits I already have hanging in my closet?" Lydia pleaded.

Sami pushed her through the door and gave her a faint smile as she hung five dresses on the hook inside the small room. She closed the door quickly and said, "I thought you'd be more

4

excited than this. Ben Markle reserved three tables and made it mandatory for the whole staff to attend. You've secured more new clients for them than the acquisition team has in their five-year existence."

Lydia slipped the skinny black dress over her head, smoothed her hands down to her waist, and sucked her breath in. The fabric clung to her curves, and she rested her hands on her lower stomach. No matter how she dressed or how far she was away from her Amish home, the small scar, only noticeable to her on her abdomen, reminded her of all she had lost. She sucked in a breath and let the memories linger just long enough to leave an aching void in her heart.

For five years, she worked hard to forget, but at night, when she was all alone, the memories of Aaron Shetler kept her awake long into the night. She fought to keep his dark brown hair and eyes fresh in her mind. After five years, it was getting harder to remember the sound of his voice or the depth of the cleft in his chin, which she imagined was now covered with a beard. She'd made so many mistakes by pushing Aaron away for the likes of Jimmy Scott. If only she could go back to the point in her life where their two paths intersected. If only she would have chosen Aaron instead.

Startled by Sami's interruption, Lydia studied the slim cocktail dress and wrapped her arms over her chest, hoping to cover herself up some.

"So?" Sami asked as she rattled the door handle. "Are you going to show me or what?"

Lydia unlocked the door and held it open, allowing Sami to view her choice. "Wow! That's perfect; you don't need to try on others."

"What? I hardly think it's appropriate." Lydia looked over her shoulder into the mirror. "And it hugs my bottom. I'm not looking to draw attention in this manner."

Sami argued. "If I had a figure like yours, I'd be doing everything possible to make a statement like that."

Lydia giggled. "Who are you trying to kid? You wouldn't be caught dead in something this tight. Your father would roll over in his grave if he caught you flashing your knees in public like this."

"Yeah, you're right. But dang, Lydia, you look great in it." Sami put her finger to her chin and said, "Wait, I have an idea."

As she waited for her to return, Lydia had to remind herself she wasn't Amish anymore, and there was no reason she couldn't wear something a little more revealing. Besides, she didn't have to worry about anyone seeing her, specifically her family. Her father and brothers had long given up on her, and the letters finally stopped begging her to return to the church to repent her sins. If it weren't for her friend, Ruthie Mast, she wouldn't know if her family were dead or alive.

Now part of the New Order Fellowship Church, Ruthie didn't heed the Old Order practices and called and wrote often. Ruthie let it slip that Aaron had married a young widow from one of the northern communities a year after she left. It took over a year for her to come to terms with that information, but to this day, the mere thought of him loving someone else still hurt.

Sami pushed her arm into the door. "Here. Maybe you'll feel more comfortable wearing this silver shrug over it."

Lydia slipped her arms into the soft fabric and twirled to see if it covered most of the tight-fitting dress from behind. "I suppose this will work."

***

Lydia and Sami entered Pittsburgh's high-end hotel and headed to the banquet hall. As they waited to check in, Lydia shifted from one foot to the other in her fashionable but uncomfortable high heels. "What I wouldn't give for flip-flops right now," she muttered.

Sami swatted her hand. "If your accent weren't so prominent, I might think you could get away with it. But one look at your bare feet and the whole place would know you're more inclined to farm than fame."

She leaned in. "What's wrong with my accent?"

"Your Pennsylvania Dutch inflection is what got you this job. For some reason, Ben picked it over my Southern drawl. He said it was a pleasant change of pace to the other voices he interviewed."

Lydia grabbed Sami's arm as she stumbled. "Bare feet have to be better than these painful heels."

Sami shushed her as they took their name tags and found their seats. After taking a sip of water from the crystal goblet, her boss, Ben Markle, rested his hand on her shoulder. Looking up at his towering frame, she sloshed water on the white linen tablecloth as she set the glass back down and twisted away from his touch.

"Tonight's your big night. Are you ready?" he muttered in her ear.

Lydia tried to keep calm, minimizing the event. "I'm happy the firm is winning such an award."

Mr. Markle squeezed her shoulder, winked, and leaned in closer. "You keep making me money hand over fist like this, and I can guarantee you'll get more than a silly award."

No matter how long she worked in the corporate world, she'd never get used to Mr. Markle's sly comments and unfitting advances. Sami and she had discussed his flirty behavior, but since he didn't act that way with Sami, they played it off as her being too sensitive to his casual touch.

Mr. Markle made his way to the podium and tapped the microphone. A murmur of hushes rippled through the crowd and a round of applause accompanied him as he beamed at the attention, warming the crowd with his wit and pizzazz before resting his eyes on Lydia. A blush rose to her face, and Lydia pulled her sweater tighter, regretting her choice of clothing. Without warning, she yearned for the safety of her Amish community. Every woman at Markle Media pined for Ben Markle's attention; but he made Lydia downright uncomfortable.

However, Sami claimed that was the nature of the business: all glam and prestige, with little truth and loyalty. From the beginning, Lydia stayed true to making her podcast guests feel comfortable despite the cutthroat media game Markle Media tried to play. Her guests never had to worry that she would surprise them with unwanted attention to their personal life and always took time to showcase their career in the utmost professional manner. She was sure that was what made her weekly podcast such a success.

Even Mr. Markle commented on her ease with the interviewing process, and her knack for asking the most interesting questions. He took an odd liking to her and often called her into his office, claiming he wanted to get to know her better. Perhaps it was all those years she helped her father run the bookshop, or maybe her love of reading helped her challenge the authors on a new, more sincere level. Whatever the reason, Ben Markle made it known he was pleased with her success.

A few seconds before Mr. Markle waved her to the front, her phone vibrated, and she turned it over on the table, but not before she saw the familiar number. It had been years since she'd seen Shetler's Amish Market's number. A flash of Aaron's face invaded her mind as she walked to the front of the crowded room.

After receiving a standing ovation, he handed her a gold plaque. When he placed the mic under her nose, she stared out over the crowd with no words to express her true feelings. After an uncomfortable silence, Mr. Markle turned on the charm as he said, "Our award winner is star-struck." He was happy enough to take credit for her successful show. He gleamed in the limelight, relieving Lydia from the attention.

Glasses raised, and Lydia returned to her seat as all started to talk and laugh amongst themselves. Mr. Markle turned the presentation over to the business association's president. He sat with some of Pittsburgh's most influential publishing giants at the table.

Without taking her seat, Lydia picked up her phone, walked out of the room, and hit redial, but as expected, the phone went to the answering machine. The number belonged to the phone at Shetler's Market, just a quarter of a mile from her childhood home. She couldn't leave a message but hoped Aaron would recognize her number on the caller ID. She slipped into the bathroom and settled into one of the overstuffed chairs, wishing Aaron would call back.

Flipping through her notifications, she saw a voice message from Ruthie. She clicked it open and hit play. "Lydia, *kemma haym,* it's your *datt.*"

She cringed as she played Ruthie's message to come home over again. An unsettled, worrisome emotion settled in her gut. When her phone buzzed, she froze and stopped breathing as she swiped the phone to answer the call.

"Aaron, is that you?"

"*Jah.* Lydia?"

"What is it? I just got a message from Ruthie too."

Aaron paused, but she could hear him take a long breath before he answered. "Lydia, it's your *datt.* I found him this morning... dead."

His soft-spoken manner helped her make sense of the words and forced her to repeat them. "Dead. You found my *datt* dead? How? Where? What happened?"

Lydia listened with alarm as Aaron explained how he had found her father huddled over his newspaper at the bookshop and how the front window was broken when he showed up to make some repairs to the bathroom.

He whispered her name when she didn't make a sound after he had given her all the information. "Lydi, are you okay?"

Just the sound of his voice as he said his pet name for her warmed a spot that had long turned cold. "*Jah,* I'm here."

When a group of women entered the bathroom, she left and found a quiet spot down the hall. With Aaron still close to her ear, her breathing took on a painful beat as she struggled to take in his words; everything rose in desperate denial. "This can't be. I didn't have a chance... a chance to say I'm sorry," she cried. "This can't be happening."

Aaron tried to comfort her, but the devastating shock of never seeing her father's face again covered her like ice. As she made her way out a set of double doors into the sweltering Pittsburgh heat, she swallowed a wave of bile and ran to her car. She ended the call with Aaron's plea to *"Kemma haym."*

***

Aaron placed the phone in the receiver and sat on a stool at the counter, the silence in his family's dry goods store amplified the wave of emotions from hearing her voice.

Memories of Lydia swirled around him, haunting every nook and cranny of the darkened store, tugging at his heart. Five years had passed since Lydia had occupied his thoughts, but the wounds she left behind became as raw as ever at that exact moment. Perhaps he should have let someone else call to tell her the news about her father, but he felt obligated since he was the one who found him. He rested his chin in his propped-up hand and sighed as the past played a story in his mind.

When she made the bold decision to walk away from her family, the church, and their shared memories, she unwittingly snatched a big piece of his heart along the way.

The rumors that filtered through the Amish grapevine haunted him for months, and it was only after he'd witnessed her with the *Englisher* boy Jimmy Scott, that the harsh truth hit him like a thunderbolt.

Any hope he clung to for a future with her vanished as swiftly as the red car she rode in, leaving him alone with just fragments of a love that was once pure and uncomplicated. The realization that she chose a different path, one that didn't involve him, stung him with bitterness that he just recognized had failed to heal over time.

***

After sending a quick text to Sami explaining her sudden departure, Lydia tossed her phone in her bag and pressed the car alarm, trying to remember where she had parked. The stagnant air in the parking garage gave her little relief as she followed the sound of her car's alarm.

Following the signs to the street, Lydia couldn't help but think of her *bruders*. The youngest and only *schwester* to seven brothers, her heart cried out for them. She hadn't heard from them in years and assumed they had written her off, much like her *datt*. Never knowing her mother, and her father not remarrying after her death, the only nurturing she had was their ill attempt at raising a little *schwester*.

Ten years her senior, Joshua, her older *bruder* took over when their mother died during childbirth delivering her. Where a mother's intuition should have kicked in during Lydia's impressionable years, books opened a world hidden to her between the pages.

The Book Cellar held different memories for her and Joshua. While her brother held onto an edge of embarrassment at their father's chosen profession, she, on the other hand, felt right at home, letting the crisp pages of a new book carry her away to forbidden possibilities.

Joshua craved the smell of freshly turned soil and a barn full of Holsteins and grumbled at having to work at the store. Only after Joshua married did his father move to the small apartment over the bookshop, allowing Joshua and his new bride, Melinda, to work the fifty acres surrounding the aging farmhouse.

Melinda tried to mold Lydia into a good Amish woman, which almost worked until her *Rumspringa*. Ignoring her sister-in-law's pleas to forgo her running around period and concentrate on Aaron Shetler's advances, she found herself intrigued with some of Willow Spring's *Englisch* teenagers. Ultimately, the lure of smartphones and cars led Lydia down a path of sin and regret.

The *Englisch* boy who forced himself on her promised her the world after the six-pack wore off. However, when she couldn't conceal her growing middle a minute longer, she tucked a goodbye note in place of a stack of twenties in her father's cash register and climbed into Jimmy's car to escape the shame of her careless actions. Two months later, she found herself on the doorstep of an unplanned pregnancy center in downtown Pittsburgh.

Turning at the sign to the apartment she shared with Sami, she followed the winding sidewalk to her assigned parking spot. Her sense of security and equilibrium was disturbed, and it took her a few minutes to gather her thoughts.

Now what? She thought. *How can I go home? Will my bruders even allow me to attend his funeral?*

As she turned the car off to put the fob in her purse, the long gold skeleton key to the bookshop caught her attention. It had become such a hidden part of her past that, most days, she paid it little thought. But now, considering her concerns, her father's apartment could welcome her home. Even if the community wouldn't.

A shower and a clean pair of jeans helped a little, but Lydia couldn't shake the dread settling on her shoulders. Finger-combing her long chestnut hair, she opened her closet and pulled out a suitcase. Without much thought, she packed, adding her one and only Amish dress to the top before zipping it closed.

Looking around her modest bedroom, she couldn't help but feel like she had never made it home. Void of any knickknacks or wall décor, it reminded her more of her simple upbringing than her trendy Pittsburgh lifestyle. On the other hand, Sami had decorated the rest of the apartment to match her Southern roots, filled with magnolia paintings, Charleston skyscapes, and a beachy color palette.

The apartment was pleasant enough, but the cost far

outweighed the need. It should have felt like home, but she never thought she belonged, even with its comfy chairs and a picture-perfect view of the Allegheny River.

When her phone buzzed and Sami's picture appeared, she swiped to answer.

"Lydia, I just saw your text. Mr. Markle is furious you left. The Pittsburgh Press wants pictures. You need to come back here, and quick!"

"Go handle it. I left the award on the table. You deserve it as much as I do."

"I got your message that you had an emergency at home, but what could be more important than your job?"

Lydia paused and forced her vocal cords to release before replying, "It's my father...they found him dead this morning."

Silence reigned on the other end for a few seconds. "Oh, Lydia, I'm so sorry. What happened?"

"I'm not sure, but I'm at the apartment packing a bag now. I'm going home."

"What should I tell Mr. Markle?"

"I really don't care. Tell him I quit." Lydia hesitated. "No, don't do that. Tell him I'll call him on Monday."

"What can I do?"

"There's nothing you can do right now but take pictures for the newspaper and calm Mr. Markle down. I'll call you in a few days once I figure out what's happening."

"But Lydia, your family? Are you sure you'll be welcomed?"

"I'm not sure. Regardless, he's still my father, and I have every right to be there."

"I'm worried about you."

"Sami, you're a good friend, and I appreciate all you've done for me. But it's time... time I face my past."

After saying goodbye, she tucked her phone in her pocket and hugged Sami's calico cat. A rescue from the Humane Society, their multi-colored house guest had become essential to their life. "You take good care of Sami, you hear?" Lydia pulled the bundle to her chest and closed her eyes, allowing his gentle purr to calm her, if only for a few minutes.

She turned to the front door and gave her apartment one last look. For some reason, she felt like she was looking at it for the last time. She mourned for only a minute before reality set in. There had been no joy in her life since she handed her daughter over to the adoption agency and walked away from the women's shelter with nothing but a GED.

Tracy Fredrychowski

CHAPTER 2

Aaron poured himself a cup of coffee and enjoyed a few lingering sips before Mattie Rose made her way downstairs. He missed his deceased wife the most in those few stolen moments of first light. Her presence lined their home the earliest, right before dawn. She loved getting up before him to ensure he had all he needed before heading to work.

When her leukemia eased its way back into their life unnoticed last year, the aggressive disease took her from him in a few short months—leaving him to raise Mattie Rose alone. He had thought of no one else until that exact moment.

He woke with Lydia on his mind. Being the one to find her father slumped over his morning paper at the bookshop left him rattled, to say the least. Wally Troyer had been a good friend and an even better customer. And when Wally decided to update the store's interior, he called Aaron first.

Well known for his handyman skills, many of the town's

business owners used him for general repairs and carpentry to the centuries-old Main Street buildings. Aaron was due to start renovations to the Book Cellar on Friday morning. Instead, he spent the morning boarding up the front glass window and answering Detective Lewis Powers' questions.

When they finally let him leave, the yellow police tape surrounded the building, and the store closed tight. However, he did make sure Wally's son Joshua was notified.

Joshua and Melinda had become good friends to him, even to the point of watching Mattie Rose when he was on a job that wasn't fit for a six-year-old to be underfoot.

Mattie Rose loved the bookshop and would have been with him any other day. But that morning, she chose to play with Joshua and Melinda's children instead.

Aaron wasn't sure he had done the right thing in contacting Lydia, but something deep inside told him to call. Not knowing how to reach her, it was only by pure luck that her contact information was written on a notepad on the table next to her father's body.

As he sat quietly waiting for Mattie Rose to wake up, his mind raced over the details that Detective Powers pointed out. Why was the front window broken out from the inside, but the door locked up tight when Aaron arrived? If there had been a robbery, wouldn't Wally have been startled? His body was found slumped over as if he'd fallen asleep reading the paper. The cherry pipe tobacco aroma was still evident on the patio when Aaron found him.

Aaron shook his head, trying to make sense of it all. He was no investigator, but nothing made sense even to his untrained eye.

The most confusing information was why Wally had Lydia's number written on his notepad. He failed to disclose that tidbit of information to Lewis, tucking the number in his pocket before he called 911.

When the county coroner refused to release Wally's body to the Troyer family upon the pending investigation, the elders held a special meeting with Lydia's brothers. Aaron was thankful it was an off-church Sunday since the community would surely discuss Wally's death instead of concentrating on the message.

As far as Aaron knew, Lydia had arrived back in Willow Springs late last night. Where she had gone, he didn't know. Perhaps to her father's apartment over the top of the bookshop or Joshua and Melinda's?

It was well known throughout the community that Wally held tight to his Old Order's position on shunning, even if most of his adult sons had switched to the New Order Fellowship, just like himself. Aaron doubted Lydia knew that most of her family had stepped away from their work-based religion and would welcome her back into their lives as their New Order Fellowship permitted.

Averting his attention, the pitter-patter of Mattie Rose's bare feet echoed above as his daughter made her way downstairs. Pettie for her age, she struggled to carry her favorite blanket, a faceless doll, and one very tattered stuffed bear, down the stairs while rubbing sleep from her eyes.

Pushing his chair away from the table, he patted his knee and invited her to his lap. "How's my girl this morning?"

Mattie Rose positioned her collection on the table and rubbed her face on his shoulder. When she lost her *mamm*, she also lost the desire to communicate. Aaron's mother insisted the girl would come around in her own time, and he wasn't to make a big deal of it. But it worried him. She would start school soon, which may be an issue if she still wasn't talking before September.

Resting his chin on Mattie Rose's head, Aaron pulled her

close to savor the joy the little girl brought him. She wiggled from his hold and pointed to the box of cold cereal on the counter just as a knock on the door announced a visitor.

Aaron glanced out the kitchen window before heading to the front room. The white police cruiser parked adjacent to the barn was why it went unnoticed. Detective Powers stood with his back to the door as Aaron pulled the door open.

Long-time friends Lewis and Aaron grew up together in Willow Springs. But again, there weren't too many *Englisch* or Amish that didn't know his father owned Shetler's Grocery.

"Lewis, what brings you out so bright and early this morning?"

Without turning to greet him, he responded, "What I wouldn't do to wake up to this each day." Lewis gazed out over the open farmland and pointed to the field of corn waving in the morning breeze.

Aaron moved to his side. "It's a lot of work, but I wouldn't trade it for anything. Coffee?"

Lewis nodded and took his hat off, following Aaron to the kitchen.

Pulling a mug and a bowl from the cupboard, Aaron asked, "Anything new with the Troyer case?"

"No, but it is the reason I stopped by. I have a few more questions to go over. Is this a good time?"

Aaron held a finger up and then pointed to Mattie before filling her bowl with milk and cereal and carrying it to the front room.

Pushing a stack of newspapers out of the way on the coffee table, he sat Mattie Rose's breakfast down, patted the top of her head, and opened a storybook to look at while she ate.

Aaron picked up his cup and rested back on the counter. "So, how can I help?"

"You know what I'm up against, right?"

Aaron nodded. "You grew up here. You didn't really think this would be different. Did you?"

"No, but I was hoping I could get the church to see my position just once. A man is dead, and conflicting circumstances have me questioning things."

"You know as well as I do that they'll never agree to an autopsy. Regardless of how things are changing here, Wally was still Old Order; to them, his death was God's will. No questions asked."

"Since there were no obvious signs of a struggle or murder, the coroner was forced to release his body to the Troyer family late last night."

Aaron took a sip from his cup. "Come on, you had to expect that."

Lewis paused to pour cream into his coffee. "I did. But I can't help having this gnawing suspicion there's more to it. Especially since you found the windows busted from the inside out."

"That's got me questioning things too. However, the front door lock was one of the things Wally wanted me to work on. Wally complained that the lock would catch and lock at will."

"That explains the door, but what about the window?"

"Can't help you with that one."

Lewis pulled a small notebook from his front pocket and clicked on his pen. "Do you mind if I ask you a few more questions, just for the record?"

Aaron took a seat at the table. "Not sure what more I can tell you. I think I told you everything on Friday."

"I know, but I need to go over it again. The chief will force me to close this case when I get to the station. No autopsy, no robbery, no case."

"But we still have the broken window that has no explanation."

"True, but that doesn't prove anything."

Aaron shook his head. "Guess not. So, what more can I tell you?"

"Let's start with what you saw when you arrived." Lewis read back over his notes before continuing. "So, you said you arrived around seven. Right?"

"Close to seven. I dropped Mattie Rose off at Melinda's first and left the house at six. That would get me to the Book Cellar a little after seven."

"Other than glass on the sidewalk, did you notice anything else that looked out of place?"

Aaron thought for a moment. "It was a quiet morning. When I turned the corner, I didn't see anyone other than a young man on a bike at the light."

"Turned the corner?"

"I walked around to the front of the building. The gate was locked on the patio, so I had no choice but to walk around to the front."

"Did you go through the gate?"

"Wally half expected me to join him for a cup of coffee on the patio when I would arrive early like that."

"And the gate was always unlocked?"

"Yes, I can't remember when I found it secured. I assumed he unlocked it when he knew I was coming."

"Why on the patio and not inside?"

Aaron chuckled. "The old man had a thing for his pipe. As long as I've known him, he started his day with a pipe of cherry tobacco, black coffee, and the newspaper. Tobacco and new books don't mesh, so he kept the smoke outside."

Lewis took notes. "I see. What can you tell me about the boy on the bike?"

"Nothing out of the ordinary. Just a tall, lanky fellow. Can't tell you much more than that."

"Amish? Wait, no bikes allowed, right?"

Aaron furrowed his eyebrows. "I think he had on a baseball cap. Yep, the *Ordnung* still prohibits bicycles in this district."

"Okay, so once you made your way to the front of the store, what did you see?"

"Glass on the sidewalk. I looked around, trying to figure out what would have broken the glass, but there was nothing but a hole in the windowpane. I knocked on the locked door, and no one answered, so I climbed in through the broken window."

"Did you see anything out of sorts when you entered the building? Try to remember exactly what you did and what you saw when you walked inside."

"When I first went in, it was dark. The building faces west, so I needed to turn on the lights. I didn't see anything out of the ordinary. I hollered out for Wally, and when he didn't answer, I made my way to the stairs that led to the cellar and the back patio."

"When you found him, did you move him at all?"

"No, like I told you on Friday, the way he was slumped over, I knew he was dead before I even checked. I did check for a pulse, and when I did, his pipe fell from his hand. The only thing I did was pick up the pipe and put it in the ashtray."

"Did you smell anything in particular?"

"Smell? I don't know. Maybe coffee and tobacco."

"Was the pipe still warm when you picked it up?"

"Not that I remember."

"I noted that his coffee cup was almost empty when I arrived." Lewis leaned back in his chair and bounced his thumbs off the chair arms. "So, if he was expecting you, why didn't he unlock the gate?"

"Got me. Perhaps he forgot, but I've known him for a long time, and he didn't falter from his routine much unless someone disrupted him."

"Anything else you can remember?"

Aaron glanced over at the slip of paper he tore from Wally's notepad. "Not sure how important it might be, but I did take this." Aaron handed Lewis the yellow slip of paper.

"Lydia's phone number and address? Where did you find it?"

"It was written on the notepad on the table next to him."

Lewis wrote her information in his notes. "I saw her at Joshua's and wondered who called her. I thought her family couldn't talk to her."

"Technically, she wasn't shunned since she never joined the church. However, Joshua and Melinda left the Old Order last year and joined the new church district. I do believe they have kept in some contact with her over the years. A few of her brothers and their families are still in the Old Order and unofficially shunned her for leaving. It's a mess for sure."

Lewis scratched his head. "I can't keep track of who is with what church. Never did understand the whole shunning thing. Seems a little extreme to me. This family member can't eat or do business with another. But this one can. Too much to keep up with even for my detail-oriented mind."

Aaron brushed his bangs off his forehead. "We're trying to

change things around here, but it's hard for the older members to conform to the new ways."

"So, if Lydia wasn't allowed to talk to her father, why would he have her number close by?" Lewis asked.

"You're the detective. I guess it's your job to figure it out. I can't help but think there's more to the story," Aaron inserted.

Lewis slid the slip of paper back across the table. "What do you think will happen to the bookshop?"

"Not sure. I can't see Joshua having any benefit in it now." Aaron stood and warmed his coffee. "Wally owned the building, so I'm sure they'll have to figure it out."

Holding his almost empty cup out for Aaron to fill, Lewis asked, "Do you think Lydia will stay to take care of it?"

The thought of Lydia remaining in Willow Springs made Aaron's heart skip a beat. "Your guess is as good as mine. Looks like the most sensible thing to do, but I'm unsure how she feels about that. She's been gone for five years, and I'm not sure some of her brothers would welcome her home."

"By the looks of it last night, Joshua didn't act like her being back was an issue. I was the one who stopped by and told them their father's body was being released today."

Mattie Rose carried in her bowl and pointed to the opened

box of cereal on the counter. Aaron poured a few oat circles in her remaining milk, and she went back to the living room.

"Cute kid. If I didn't know better, I'd think she was yours." Aaron winced at his friend's comment and snapped back, slapping the spot over his heart. "She's mine where it counts."

"Hey man, I didn't mean anything by it. I'm sure Mattie Rose doesn't even remember her biological father, and you've been all she's known since her own father died when she was so young. I know how you and Frannie wanted one of your own, even before she got sick."

Aaron set his cup in the sink. "I'm just sorry Frannie didn't live long enough to see how great she is."

Lewis stood, pushed his chair in, put back on his hat, and headed to the door. "If you think of anything else, let me know. The station might close this case, but I won't write it off completely. Right now, all I have to go on is a broken window. Certainly not enough to warrant an investigation."

Aaron followed him to the door and waved him off before shutting the door and turning toward Mattie Rose. "Well, kiddo, what should we do today?"

Mattie Rose held up her book, turned to the page where a bear was eating ice cream, and pointed to the picture.

"It's too early for ice cream, but maybe we can ride into town this afternoon." He tousled her hair and instructed. "How about you get dressed while I do chores? I'm sure Stout would like some breakfast too."

Mattie Rose shot up and ran to the stairs. He knew if anything would light a fire under his slowpoke little girl, a chance to visit with her favorite pony would do the trick.

After carrying her bowl to the kitchen, he tucked Lydia's number in his pocket. At some point, he'd need to stop by the bookshop to pick up his tools and see if she wanted him to finish what her father started.

As he strode outside, a row of brown-topped buggies clip-clopped past the house. Five, to be exact, all headed to Joshua and Melinda's across Willow Bridge Road with Lydia's older *bruders* and their families in tow.

CHAPTER 3

It took a few moments for Lydia to realize where she was. The fresh bread and strong coffee aroma made their way under the door in Joshua and Melinda's spare room. It had taken her hours to fall asleep in the muggy upstairs. Even with both windows open, the air failed to offer relief, making her wish for her air-conditioned apartment. When she rolled over to face the stream of sunshine invading her morning, she watched as a trapped fly bounced against the screen. Momentarily, she felt the fly's pain of being caught in an unfamiliar place and looking for any way to escape.

Before she moved her feet to the floor, her legs felt wobbly. The strain of facing her eldest *bruder* the night before left a lasting effect. Harvey's reaction shouldn't have surprised her; he had always been cranky and opinionated. Her senior of thirty years, Harvey made it clear where he stood with her arrival back in Willow Springs. He'd been old enough to be her father when

35

she was born, a shock to everyone, arriving when her mother was fifty, upsetting the family dynamics.

Her siblings had little to do with her since most were already married before she came along. They were unaware of her sensitivity to their remarks about her being the cause of their mother's death. Even though she knew her parents, as did every other Amish family, accepted children as God's gifts, regardless of when or how they arrived. Unaware of how their comments bore a hole in her heart, she'd grown up feeling less than loved; a nuisance at best to her *bruders*. If it weren't for the gentleness of Joshua, who favored their *datt*, she might have disappeared into the woodwork without any of them noticing she was gone.

It could be why, when some of the teenagers who came into the bookshop paid attention to her, she jumped at the chance to have some friends her own age. The jarring ring of her cell phone made her jump from the past to the present instantly as she tried to quiet it.

"Lydia, you didn't call last night. I was worried." Sami exclaimed.

Lydia propped back against her pillows, comforted by Sami's familiar voice. "I'm sorry. Some of my brothers were here, and it was anything but easy."

"Where's here?"

"Joshua and Melinda's."

"They let you in? I wasn't sure they'd welcome you."

"No, Joshua is wonderful. He and Melinda belong to a New Order Fellowship now, and they don't practice shunning like some of my brothers still do."

"Thank goodness. I never will understand how a family can just write you off like that." Sami waited, and when Lydia didn't comment, she continued, "And your dad? Do they know how he died?"

"No one is sure. Joshua said he was in perfect health."

"Now what? Do you know how long you'll be staying?"

"I'm not sure. His funeral is tomorrow. It'll be here at Joshua and Melinda's. This was his farm until he moved above the bookshop. Since he was an active member of the Old Order, my being here is causing some stress among my older brothers."

Sami sighed. "But he was still your dad, and you have every right to be there. Don't you?"

"It's complicated. I'm sure no one is going to push me away, but I may have to stay in the back and not go out of my way to talk to anyone."

"I'm sorry, Lydia; I know that must be hard. Hey...I called because you got a package yesterday. Do you want me to send it to you?"

"That's strange. I wasn't expecting anything. Who's it from?"

"Doesn't say, but it's postmarked Willow Springs."

"If it's not too much trouble, do you mind?"

"Not at all. I'll do it during my lunch hour tomorrow. Where should I send it?"

After giving Sami the address to the bookshop, she hung up and wandered to the window that overlooked her *bruder's* farm. The view held many memories, all circling back to Aaron Shetler. From where she stood, she could see the banks of Willow Creek that butted up against the field that separated the house from the Shetler's property, just a half mile down Spring Quarry Road that turned into South Main Extension at the creek.

With the morning sun streaming through the window, she watched her *bruders* buggies pulling into the driveway. Today was the day her family prepared for her father's funeral that would be held the following day.

***

Lydia tugged at her too-snug jeans and stopped as a mixture of longing and excitement dawned in stages as she watched Aaron walk across the yard. She took a gulp of air, and time seemed to stop as the earth around her moved slowly; he removed his hat and asked, "How are you? Are your *bruders* making things difficult for you?"

"*Nee*, not too much. Joshua is shielding me from much of it, I'm sure." She paused and let years' worth of silence fall between them. "*Denki* for calling."

"*Jah*."

"Joshua said you'd been helping *Datt* do some repairs to the store."

Aaron nodded. "He'd been having some trouble with the plumbing. I've been replacing the old pipes and fixtures."

Lydia's heart swelled at the thought of her father asking for his help. Aaron's quiet and gentle manner had always been a cornerstone of her youth, and even now, she yearned for the closeness they once shared. If only she had listened to him, heeding his warning about the crowd she hung out with, things would have turned out differently for both of them. "I'm sorry about Frannie. I had no idea until Melinda told me yesterday that she had passed."

Aaron's face took on a solemn gaze. "God's will. Much like your *datt. Jah?*"

"Jah. But it doesn't make either any easier."

"Nee. But life goes on."

Ruthie called to her from across the yard. "I best go see what she needs. I'm going to stay in the apartment over the shop. Will I have any trouble with the plumbing?"

"You shouldn't, but I'll stop by this week and finish what I was supposed to take care of on Friday."

Aaron had always been an immovable part of Lydia's life. From her earliest memory, he was always present. As she walked away, she fought to keep herself from turning back and the old feelings from returning to the surface of her heart.

***

Ruthie rested her hand on Lydia's forearm. "I've been looking for you. You'll never believe what I just overheard."

"I'm afraid to hear," Lydia mumbled.

"Edna and Melinda were arguing about you of all things."

Ruthie rested her hands on her hips and resumed. "Just the thought of it and only hours from laying your *datt* to rest."

Lydia glanced toward the house. "I can only imagine. Edna and Harvey aren't too happy I'm here. Seems I've disturbed the apple cart some. I'm trying to stay out of their path as much as possible." Lydia guided Ruthie away from the house. "Perhaps I shouldn't have come."

"Don't be silly! You have every right to be here. And besides, tensions are high right now. I'm sure things will calm down in a few days."

"I'm not too sure of that. Harvey's still pretty upset that I took off like I did."

"While I may disagree with how you went about it, I understand why you left. Harvey might have understood more if he knew what you were facing."

"Oh... heaven's no, I could have never told him what I'd done."

Ruthie exhaled a long breath, turned toward Lydia, and said, "There's more than one secret in most families, and I can only bet most of your *bruders* have some of their own."

Ruthie's pitch softened. "I'm so sorry about your *datt*."

"I'm fine, really. It was his time to go, and nothing I could have done could stop God's will." Lydia mumbled. "Maybe some good will come out of me coming home."

Ruthie looped her arm in Lydia's. "You'd be surprised at what God can do. He restored my family and can do the same for you."

"You have more faith than I do." Lydia stared across the yard toward the picnic table where her family had settled under the shade of the maple tree. "I feel like such an outsider. I really don't belong here anymore."

Ruthie leaned in and breathed, "God's healing power is at work. Look at your *bruders'* families. Most have left the Old Order and embraced the New Order Fellowship. If that isn't God's power working, I'm unsure what is. You won't feel like you belong until you try."

"I suppose you're right." Lydia sighed.

Ruthie gently touched Lydia's back and pressed her toward her family. "God is in the business of taking broken families and making them whole. It's never too late to let God heal what's broken in your family."

As Lydia walked across the yard, she recalled a time when she'd lay on the picnic table in the middle of the night, trying to escape the smoldering heat of her upstairs bedroom. The cicadas kicked up a deafening racket in the fields surrounding her father's farm, lulling her to sleep. It was nights like that when she dreamed of the mother she never knew, trying to imagine what she looked like or how she might smell and the sound of her voice. But no matter how hard she tried; a clear vision never came to mind.

Now, as she made her way across the yard, she ached for the mother she never got a chance to know. Someone who would welcome her home only like a mother could.

Suddenly, a searing pain slashed through her chest with a haunting question driving a knife into her heart. Would her own daughter dream of the same things one day? As the agonizing choice to not keep her infant daughter lingered, she couldn't help but wonder if the cycle of regret was destined to repeat itself.

In a barely audible mummer, she fought through the thick air to ask herself, "What is it about this place that's making me doubt my past decisions?" The words escaped her lips like a desperate plea, begging to make sense of an array of unresolved emotions.

When Melinda moved over and patted the seat next to her on the bench, Lydia forced the lump in her throat down and smiled. *"Denki."*

"Your *bruders* have been looking for you."

"For what?" she muttered.

"I'm not sure, but it has something to do with the bookshop. Joshua went back in the house looking for you."

Lydia bent in and whispered," Ruthie said you were arguing with Edna. Was it about me being here?"

"Don't you worry, I can manage Edna. She feeds off Harvey and tries to stir up trouble whenever possible."

"I'm sorry I've caused so much trouble."

"The only trouble you're causing is worrying about such things. Now stop." Melinda patted her knee under the table and muttered. "Do you see anyone else at this table upset with you being here?"

"Nee."

"Exactly. Once this week is over, you won't see much of them. They'll return to their farms and their *g'mays* and leave you alone." Melinda tilted in even closer. "Joshua says Harvey likes to be boss and likes to be heard. I suspect Edna comes by it naturally after being married to him for so long."

Lydia's lips turned upward. "I'll take your word for it."

Melinda lifted her head toward Joshua and Harvey heading

her way. "I suspect they've come looking for you."

Lydia squeezed Melinda's hand. "Lord, help me." She laughed, but her smile faded when Harvey's chin tilted in a sour manner.

Joshua spoke. "Lydia, may we have a word with you?"

Lydia looked down the table at her *schwesters-in-law*, hoping their presence would shield her from harsh words. "*Jah.*"

"Perhaps in private?"

"Whatever you must say, you can say it here. We're all family, aren't we?"

Joshua looked back at Harvey and then back toward her, pausing before he replied, "We need your help."

"Help? With what?"

Joshua spoke earnestly. "We haven't decided what to do about the bookshop yet. Seems like some of *Datt's* papers are missing, and until we can locate them, we need someone to look after the store."

"Papers?"

"Nothing you need to concern yourself with. But we'll need to keep the store open until we find what he'd done with them."

"For how long? I do have a job I'll need to get back to."

Joshua looked at Harvey, raising his brow in question. When Harvey lifted his chin and looked away, Lydia knew he refused to answer since he still considered her a threat to their values since jumping the fence to the *Englisch* side.

She stood and walked toward Harvey with all the courage she could gather. As she got closer, he turned and refused to look her in the eye. "Me being here is hard. I understand that, but I don't understand how I'm good enough to help at the store but not good enough to be spoken to like a member of this family."

When she stepped closer, he jerked away before her fingertips landed on his arm. In a quieter tone, she inserted, "It hurts me when you treat me this way. Can't you see past the old ways just this once and at least look at me?"

Without a word, he walked away, and she turned to face her other six *bruders*. "I'll stay for a few weeks until things get sorted out."

Joshua countered, "Don't let Harvey get to you. He has his own burdens to bear."

Melinda stood and stepped beside her. "You're welcome to say here as long as you like."

"*Denki*, but it would be better if I stayed at the store. At least

I can work from there if need be."

Lydia couldn't help but glance back at Harvey and Edna, making their way back into the house. It was as if all her childhood hurts came back at once, and she was sideswiped by an overwhelming sadness. Did she do the right thing in coming back? If her *bruder* couldn't stand the sight of her, what made her think the Willow Springs citizens, who were mainly Amish, would welcome her back as well?

***

Even though Aaron was too far away to hear the exchange, he couldn't help but notice Lydia's composure as she stood beside Harvey. He held his breath as she squared her shoulders and lifted her chin to his towering form. Five years was a long time to remember precisely how she carried herself into battle.

Long before she'd let tears fall, she'd stand tall and face her adversary straight on. He'd been on the receiving end on more than one occasion and flashed a grin at the memory. Her tiny five-foot-two frame was no match for her determination when she felt she'd been wronged.

He could only imagine what words rushed out as he viewed

her mouth move. He knew she'd learned early on that she had to stand tall when it came to her *bruders*, mainly when she had no *mamm* to soften their blows.

Unsettled at the display, he moved away and prayed she'd be strong enough to withstand Harvey Troyer's harsh treatment. Where time often relaxes a stubborn man, in this case, word told, Harvey Troyer got meaner and meaner with each passing year.

***

Entering the bookshop was easy enough, he'd done it many times. Using a flashlight to guide his way, he slithered through the rows of books looking for any clues to what he was looking for.

He was confident what he was after wasn't at the store. He'd already looked once, but he'd look again. Whatever was in the old man's journal was necessary, and he was determined to find it to lay claim to the crisp hundred-dollar bill waved under his nose earlier that day.

Why anyone thought old man Troyer was a threat was beyond him. For all he knew, the man kept to himself. He rarely left the store except to attend church and occasionally visit the Mercantile. In fact, as much time as he'd spent at the bookshop, he never heard him say a cruel word to anyone. Except for that one time last week when his oldest son, Harvey, came in ranting about something. He tried to listen, but they took their argument to the cellar and onto the patio downstairs.

But tonight, his job was to scour every corner, looking for something that wasn't there. And if he did find it, he'd be the first to look inside to see what was so darn important. This was the last chance he'd have to tear the place apart before Lydia moved into the apartment upstairs. He'd overheard as much just that afternoon at the funeral.

He grinned at his knack for being seen but not detected as he shone the light around the dark room. His stealthy way of blending in came in handy on more than one occasion over the last few years, and he had made a name for himself in the dark circles of Willow Springs. He was the first person most contacted if something needed to be found—or erased.

Making his way up the creaky steps to the street-level bookshop and then to the upstairs apartment, he couldn't help but pat the small notebook he carried in his back pocket. The tattered pad, held together by a thick rubber band, had more dates and facts about some of Willow Springs' upstanding business leaders to keep him in fast cash for years. He tucked the notebook tighter in his pocket and laughed at his ready-made savings plan.

Holding the small penlight between his teeth, he slipped on a pair of rubber gloves and started to look through every corner of the old man's place. This time, he didn't care to be so careful.

CHAPTER 4

L ydia pulled her car into an open parking spot across the street from the Book Cellar. Taking a silent breath and holding tight to the steering wheel, she allowed a flood of memories to invade the space between the car and the store.

The last few days had been a challenge facing so many familiar faces from a life she thought she left behind. The emptiness of their greetings left her feeling like a stranger peering into a world that no longer mirrored her own. The recent ordeal of her father's funeral drained her both emotionally and physically, leaving her with a weariness she hadn't felt in years.

She didn't know how long she sat in her car, letting the memories float in through the open window and sticking to her like a wool coat in the middle of summer. They came in flashes, reminding her of the early years when she was still young enough to enjoy being surrounded by all those books and new adventures, bringing warmth to her heart. She loved chatting with the customers, the excitement of new shipments, and having her *datt* all to herself in their cozy upstairs apartment.

But at some point, it wore off when she traded the written word for the sweet lure of Jimmy Scott. When her fascination with blue jeans and Jimmy's red Camaro won her over, she found every chance she could to escape the safety of her father's home. Like every other Amish parent in her *g'may*, her *datt* turned a blind eye to her *running around* period. Relying on prayer to lead her back into the fold.

She removed the keys from the ignition and rubbed the tarnished skeleton key between her fingers. The century-old brick building that her father owned stood nestled between The Amish Baker and the Restaurant on the Corner. Nothing had changed since she'd left, and flashes of recollections surfaced as she looked down toward the Mercantile and Sandwich Shoppe. The Book Cellar had been a fixture in the downtown community long before she was born, and the sudden death of its owner was sure to leave a lasting hole in the Amish business community.

The cobble lined streets around the bookshop raised her. While her friends were tied to farms, she was allowed to explore Willow Springs with a child's eye. And in the evening, she would curl up on her *datt's* lap as he read her story after story. When they opened the books, magic happened. His voice echoed in her ear as she recalled him whispering... *You're never alone when you read a book.*

Between the pages, her father would make the characters come to life, enticing her to engross herself in the storyline. It was there she fell in love with reading, tucked safely in her father's arms. Even the comfortable scent of his pipe tobacco and his long, scratchy beard tickling her cheek taught her kindness through example and a love for the written word.

Where her *bruders*, except for Joshua, treated her with contempt, her father showed nothing but love and compassion. And at that exact moment, she missed him like never before. It took a few minutes before she got brave enough to leave her car to walk across the street to unlock the heavy wood door.

The front window, covered with plywood, housed a handwritten note stating the shop would be closed until the following Monday.

The street was empty except for a few bank tellers leaving the Sandwich Shoppe. As the aroma of fresh bread and strong coffee lingered down the street, Lydia held her hand on the doorknob and turned the key. Fumbling to light the room, she let out a long breath as the shop came alive when the old chandelier in the entryway flickered to life. An overwhelming sense of peace traveled up her chest as she walked to the checkout counter to flip on another set of lights. The light illuminated the hallway, and the rows of bookshelves at the back of the store glowed.

The familiar scent of new books triggered a cascade of memories. Yankee, her father's loyal charcoal lab, used to greet her at the door with enthusiasm. She half-expected to see him running to her but nothing but silence greeted her. A wave of loneliness washed over her, and she yearned for the comforting touch of the dog and the gentle thud of his tail against the floor and the warmth of his companionship. She couldn't help but wonder what may have happened to the old dog.

As she walked around to the back of the counter, she tripped over a pile of books and papers scattered on the floor. She stopped to gather up the mess when a note in her father's handwriting caught her attention. She ran her finger over his perfect penmanship, realizing him being gone was still too enormous to grasp.

It was like she was swimming through a muck of guilt and grief, trying to keep from drowning. If only she had stayed and faced her mistakes. Instead, she ran and hid her shame from her father and the boy she truly loved.

The crack finally opened, and she fell back, hid her face in her hands, and let her heart shatter. Thirty minutes later, her body ached from the aftershock of her emotional outburst. She had not been prepared for how hard it was to step back into a life she could no longer share with her father.

Blowing her nose, she wondered if her father had felt the same shock wave when he realized she'd run away. A pain between her eyes made her flinch with a new surge of sadness.

The many letters he wrote, none of which she replied to, expressed how much he loved her. But she never let him know how badly she wanted to return home. Every time she came close to returning, the mere thought of the disappointment in his eyes stopped her.

Lydia felt nauseated, and her throat clogged with more inexpressible grief. Her hands shook as she pulled herself back up to the counter. All alone, she wandered to the back of the shop and into the bathroom tucked under the stairs. After splashing water on her face, she stopped to listen to a songbird. Confused at its clear sound, she returned to the hallway and followed its voice down the cellar stairs.

Lydia nearly stumbled again as she stepped over a pile of books and felt a slight breeze flitter across her face. The initial comfort she felt when she first walked into the bookshop turned into panic with the open window and another strewed mess on the floor. Her knees would have buckled if it weren't for the chills rolling up the back of her neck. Something wasn't right. She locked the window and ran back up the stairs to secure the front door.

Scrambling for her phone at the bottom of her purse, she took the stairs two at a time to the upstairs apartment. Trying to capture a sense of calm, she sighed as she pushed the door open. Light filtered into the sparsely furnished room, enough to see her father's home was ransacked even worse than downstairs.

After dialing 911, she sank into her father's chair. For her, nothing would ever be the same. When she entered the shop less than an hour earlier, she felt she was back where she belonged. But now, in the aftermath of her grief and the violation of her father's things, she felt an emptiness so vast she almost couldn't breathe. An exhausting gloom hovered over her, and she wasn't sure she was strong enough to escape it.

***

After an hour of questions and inspections, Detective Powers handed Lydia his card. "If you come up with anything missing, call me."

"Like I said, it's been nearly five years since I've been in the shop or my father's home. I wouldn't know what was missing."

The detective clipped his pen back into his shirt pocket. "Again, if I had to guess, it was a bunch of kids. The community knew your father had died, and no one would be in the shop. We've been having trouble with vandalism. Nothing was stolen, just destroyed. No rhyme or reason other than too much time with unsupervised kids and not enough to do in a small town like this."

Regardless, she locked the door after he left and headed back upstairs. A knock on the front door startled her before she made it to the top of the stairs. *Another nosy business neighbor, no doubt,* she thought. The boarded-up front window hid the visitor from view, and she had to unlock the door. When she opened the door, Aaron's brown eyes and concern etched forehead looked back at her.

"Lydia, what's going on? I was at the Feed & Seed and overheard someone mention the police were here again."

Taking one look up and down the sidewalk, she waved him in and bolted the door behind her. "Seems like someone broke in last night. God only knew what they were looking for. I can't tell if anything was stolen. But they sure did make a mess upstairs."

She'd been in a fog for the last hour and pointed to the two chairs under the boarded-up window. Uncomfortable, as if they were strangers in an overcrowded room, she studied his face and hoped he'd speak so she didn't have to think first.

"How did they get in? I'm sure I set the deadbolt on Friday when I left."

"A window in the cellar was open when I got here this morning."

He stood, and she sat motionless. "Let me go check all the windows."

She didn't argue and muttered a reserved "*Denki*" as he headed to the cellar.

After he left, she rubbed her eyes, sat on the steps, and looked around the shop. Every corner seeped a new memory, and when they wouldn't stop, she headed to the counter. Hoping to rectify the intruder's mess, she pushed aside the invasion only to have thoughts of Aaron occupy her mind. While he seemed to be generally concerned about her well-being, there was an aloofness to his manner that she no doubt deserved.

***

By two o'clock, he had installed the new locks, secured the windows overlooking the cellar patio, and supervised the installation of a new front window. Lydia had restored order to the bookshop and was working on cleaning up the mess in the apartment when he showed up at her side with takeout from the Restaurant on the Corner. Clearing a spot on the cluttered kitchen table, she invited him to sit.

Following his lead, she bowed her head and didn't lift it until he cleared his throat. "Didn't take you long to make things right in here," he stated.

"*Jah*. All that's left is the bedroom. They even went through my old things. Not sure what they hoped to find in there, there was nothing but some old dresses and dishes in my hope chest to sort through."

"Have you been able to figure out if anything is missing?"

She shrugged her shoulders. "I wouldn't know. *Datt* wasn't a collector of anything other than some old books and as far as

I can tell, they're all still in the case in the basement where he always kept them."

After taking a few bites of her sandwich, Lydia leaned back in her chair and with a crack in her voice, stated, "The shop looks the same. It's like he just went out for a bite and didn't return."

She pointed to the stack of books near his chair. "It was strange that the pile of books wasn't toppled over. His place is still marked in each one."

Aaron set his sandwich down and walked to examine the pile. "*The Fiery Trial.* This is a good one. It's about how slavery ended and Abraham Lincoln's role in it. And this one, William Faulkner's *Absalom*. He talks about what really happened in the Civil War."

"*Jah*, he always was fascinated with that time period," she commented.

"Me too." Aaron inserted as he leafed through one of the books. "We sat outside just last week and talked long about these books." Aaron stopped and looked under the stand next to his chair and into the cracks of the easy chair. "I wonder what he did with the one he was currently reading. He was most excited about that one."

"Was it about the Civil War?"

"*Nee*, it was about the underground railroad that ran through Lawrence County. I can't remember the title."

"I do," Lydia uttered. "It was one of his favorites, *In Hot Pursuit*. He was convinced this building had connections to the underground railroad. We read it together. It was boring, but he enjoyed all that history, and I loved listening to his voice as he told me all he knew about how the slaves used it to escape." Lydia brushed crumbs from the table in her hand and resumed. "I bet he read it half a dozen times."

Aaron returned to his sandwich. "I'm surprised it's not with those books. It was all he could talk about last week."

After taking a long sip of her tea, she said, "It's probably downstairs somewhere. He liked to read between customers."

"Did he ever find proof about the railroad?" Aaron asked.

"Not that I know of." Lydia dropped her head and muttered, "But again, I've not talked to him in forever." A stab of regret pierced her heart, and Aaron must have noticed since he spoke tenderly.

"Don't dwell on the past, Lydia," his voice wavered on the edge of broken promises.

Lydia's chest tightened. *Stop! Breathe, don't cry,* she

thought. Before she could respond, he scrunched up his sandwich paper and tossed it in the trash. "I best go fetch Mattie Rose from Melinda's." His abrupt departure left her with a lingering ache, a void of unspoken words.

She followed him downstairs with an air of tension between them. As he reached for his toolbelt, he turned to her and paused, struggling to form the words weaving across his lips. In a whisper, he said, "It's good that you're home, Lydi."

After bolting the door, she supported herself on the sturdy wood. The burden of the secret she carried pressed down on her shoulders as she slid to the floor. Her heart picked up pace with the anguish of her unspoken confession, and she couldn't escape the haunting fear that no one would forgive her for the choices she made so many years ago.

Resting her forehead on her knees, she breathed into the emptiness. "I gave my child away." The words hung in the air, full of regret and the fear of judgment. "I'm sorry, *Datt*, I just couldn't face you." The bookshop seemed to surround her with a warm hug as a ray of sun filtered through the rows and rows of books.

***

Aaron stood on the other side of the door with a heavy heart. The store door, an impenetrable barrier, held his own unspoken confessions of guilt and regret.

Turning to lay his hand on the polished oak, his thoughts swirled with an admission he longed to make. He blamed himself for letting her slip away and succumbed to the accusing whispers among the People. Instead of confronting her, he chose to pull away rather than jeopardize his reputation. In doing so, it cost him his heart.

Leaning against the opposite side of the door, he finally let his guard down and mouthed as if the closed door could carry his words through the invisible divide. "Lydi, I should have run after you. I should have fought harder against the gossip that tore us apart." He sighed and walked toward his buggy parked across the street. Once he climbed inside, he sat and mumbled more confessions. "I married Frannie not out of love but to hide the pain of losing you," he whispered each word in a painful acknowledgment of the dull existence he had built for himself.

Regret clawed at him as he continued, "I should have protected you from the outside world, but all I did was push you further into it." He snapped the reins and clicked his tongue as he pulled his buggy into the street.

Despite the guilt that threatened to suffocate him, he knew he couldn't fathom opening his heart to the pain again. He had Mattie Rose to think about now, a harsh reminder of the choices that had shaped his life. The thought of unraveling the wounds of the past, especially when his daughter was still hurting from the loss of Frannie, seemed like an insurmountable challenge.

***

Somewhere in the distance, a rooster crowed his good morning wishes. A slight smile landed on Lydia's lips as she welcomed the beautiful sound without opening her eyes. Forgetting to pull the shades the night before, the sun streamed through the screened window.

Her childhood bed helped her embrace a good night's sleep as the previous day's events faded. Rolling over and peering out the long, narrow second-floor window, she took in the hills winding against the sky of her hometown behind the row of businesses that lined Main Street.

She made her way to the bathroom and felt the floor give a little under her bare feet as she stood at the sink. Making a mental note to talk to Aaron about the soft spot, she pulled on a pair of jeans and pulled her hair back in a ponytail. Something about the tight fabric made her self-conscious, and she traded the faded denim for a gauzy skirt.

With the apartment all in order, she headed downstairs just as a knock at the front door echoed through the hallway.

As she unlocked the door, the mailman held out a package and a stack of mail for her to retrieve. Before she could shut the door, Aaron pulled up to the open parking spot in front of the store.

Lydia walked closer to the buggy. "What has you both out and about so early?"

Aaron glanced at Mattie Rose. "We have a breakfast date at the Sandwich Shoppe every Wednesday morning."

Lydia's lip turned upward at his obvious affection toward the little girl. "And what's your favorite?" she asked Mattie Rose.

When the child didn't answer, she asked, "Do they still have French toast sticks?"

Mattie Rose leaned closer to Aaron and buried her head into his side. "She doesn't talk much."

"That's okay; I don't like to talk much either," Lydia replied.

He gave a wry laugh. "What I wouldn't do to hear her mutter a few words." He lovingly poked Mattie Rose's side. "Isn't that right, little one?"

Lydia looked at him curiously.

"Hasn't spoken a word in over a year."

The noise from the street prevented them from speaking for a few moments but gave Lydia enough time to study the little girl. Her long blonde braids hung over her shoulders, and a little blue scarf was tied snuggly under her chin.

Her bare feet barely hung over the edge of the bench seat, and she held tightly to a tattered bear. When Lydia's glances made the young child snuggle in closer to Aaron, she closed her eyes and turned away from Lydia.

An awkward silence surrounded them, and he stated, "I left my drill inside, and I was hoping I could pick it up."

"I saw it on the counter. Wait, I'll go get it for you." As she walked back inside, she couldn't help but remember the words Melinda had murmured in her ear on the day of her father's funeral. *I promise you that the Lord has not abandoned you, and I can't help but think he sent you home for a reason.* Lydia shook her head and tried not to let Aaron's presence tug at a heart that had no plans to remain in Willow Springs.

***

Edna filled Harvey's coffee cup and rested her hand on his shoulder. "Now Harvey, calm down; you don't know for sure that's what your *datt* intended to do with the bookshop."

Harvey twisted, forcing Edna's hand to drop. "There was no talking him out of it. I had to step in. He left me no choice."

Edna pulled out a chair and joined him at the table. "There's always a choice. You could have explained things to your *bruders* before it got this far and maybe you could have come up with a solution together."

Harvey slapped a hand on the table, making Edna jump. "After all these years, I'd think you wouldn't challenge my decisions on such things."

Reaching over to lay a calming hand on his forearm, she reassured him. "I'm not. It's just that he's dead now, and there's nothing you can do but find another way. I don't think your *bruders* will ever agree to what you're proposing, especially now that Lydia's back. The store meant too much to your father to carry out your plans."

Harvey took a profound breath, trying to calm his frustration as the bitter taste of regret lingered in his coffee. Edna was right, there was no turning back time. Memories of the argument he had with his father flooded his mind. The old man adamantly declared that selling the old building was the last thing he would agree to no matter the cost. Harvey's resentment simmered beneath the surface as his father refused to listen to reason.

A pang of guilt, cold and unforgiving, now wrapped itself around him in recognition of his outburst. The weight of his words weighed heavy on his shoulders and morphed into a reality too painful to bear. Regardless, he would need to find his father's journal if he had any hope of salvaging any of his plans.

***

Ed Glick stepped back as Lydia approached the counter at the Sandwich Shoppe. Far enough to stay hidden but close enough to hear the conversation she was having with Ruthie Mast, owner of The Amish Baker.

"Like it or not, I'll need to open the bookshop on Monday." Lydia admitted, her voice carrying a mix of submission and grit.

Ruthie offered a hopeful smile. "So, you're staying?"

Lydia met Ruthie's gaze. "What choice do I have? None of my *bruders* has any concern for the store and until they decide what to do, they expect me to take care of things."

"Do you think they'll sell? The bookshop has been such an important asset to our town, I can't imagine your family not owning it."

Lydia's shoulders slumped slightly as she pondered the outcome. "Who knows? They all seem to be at odds over it, and I'm just trying to stay out of the way. Particularly Harvey. He can barely look at me without growling. He's not happy I'm back, that's for sure and certain."

Ed's lips curled into a smirk as he kept himself from being noticed. That's what he did. He faded into the background and observed people from a far, and he was mighty good at it.

Hidden behind a stack of takeout containers, he glanced back toward Lydia. The way her shoulders sank when she mentioned the bookshop prompted him to study her body language more closely.

It had been years since he'd laid eyes on Lydia Troyer, and in that moment, she appeared more alluring than he remembered. He withdrew his notebook out of his back pocket, jotted down a few notes, and stole one last lingering glance at her long brown hair and fair skin before returning to the grill. The memory of her dismissive attitude toward his past advances crawled its way through his thoughts and he found himself unable to shake the haunting image of her captivating face. He tucked the tattered notebook in his pocket and sneered under his breath. "There's more than one way to get your attention, Miss Troyer, and I'm about to become your worst nightmare." The dangerous promise lingered in the air, a faint warning to the storm Ed was about to unleash.

CHAPTER 5

L ydia pulled her hair back in a ponytail and quickly looked at herself in the reflection of the front window's glass before venturing outside. She picked up her keys and the list she had made for Aaron from the counter and marched outside. The hot Sunday afternoon left Main Street quiet from everyday busyness and helped calm her apprehension about driving to Aaron's.

As she drove toward the backroads of Willow Springs, the sun painted a picturesque landscape over the open fields, waving with the emerging tasseled corn. Pulling into Aaron's driveway, the crunch of gravel under her tires echoed the nervous rhythm of her heart. Making her way to the front porch, she hesitated before knocking on the wooden door, uncertainty gnawing at her.

The door creaked open, and Aaron's eyes met hers, his appearance guarded. A sudden hint of anxiety tightened Lydia's chest. "I hope I'm not interrupting anything," she began, tingling with hesitation.

Before Aaron had a chance to answer, a familiar sound reached her ears—the soft padding of paws on the porch. Lydia turned to see Yankee, her father's lab, emerging from the shadows, his tail wagging a warm welcome. She welcomed him with a warm hug and let him snuggle his muzzle against her cheek in a familiar hello.

Aaron glanced at Yankee, then back at Lydia. "He remembers you," he remarked, a hint of warmth breaking through. "You want to take him back with you while you're here?"

Lydia's heart skipped a beat at the offer, and she found herself struggling between the responsibilities awaiting her at the bookshop and a little part of her father Yankee represented. "You don't think it will confuse him too much?" she asked.

"Dogs are simple creatures, Lydia. They only care about sensing love and being fed. The familiar surrounding will do him good, and he'll appreciate the break from Mattie Rose treating him like a pony."

His words were packed with a truth that gave her clarity as she knelt to pet the dog, his eyes reflecting an unwavering trust.

Yankee, with his warm presence, would offer her some comfort that she yearned for in her father's apartment. When she stood, Aaron looked at her and offered a polite nod, his eyes flickering with caution. "Is there something you need?"

Lydia took a shallow breath, gathering the courage to express her request. "I was wondering if you would be interested in helping me with some repairs to the bookshop."

Aaron's response was guarded, and Lydia sensed he was struggling with accepting her offer. "I'm not sure I'm the right person to help you." He waited and looked back over his shoulder toward Mattie Rose. "I have quite a few jobs already lined up for the next couple of weeks, and I have to think about leaving Mattie Rose with sitters too much."

Trying to hide her disappointment, she was quick to add. "You can always bring her with you. I'm sure she would love the kid's corner full of books, and I don't mind keeping an eye on her for you." A heaviness settled in her chest. "But if it's too much to ask, I understand. I just thought maybe—"

"Lydia," he interrupted, his tone softening. "I'm not sure it's wise for us to spend so much time together."

The unspoken words hung in the air—an obvious tension about their unresolved past between them. A rising ache of vulnerability settled in the back of her throat, and she muttered, "I didn't mean to impose; I just don't know who—"

"It's not that I don't want to help. It's just...things have changed, and I have responsibilities to Mattie Rose now. I'm not certain how your worldly influence may affect her."

Lydia's heart sank as the truth resonated through his words. He didn't trust that she could keep the gap between their world separated. "Aaron, I... I don't want to upset you or influence Mattie Rose in any manner. But I need your help, and I hoped we could put the past behind us."

His gaze remained distant, her attention tethered to the sweet smell of fresh-cut hay wafting in the air as he said, "I can't risk getting close to you again if you're going to pick up and leave in a few weeks."

Aaron's admission mirrored her own, and an understanding silence settled between them. Perhaps she shouldn't have come and put him on the spot like she had, but she couldn't let go of the pressing need for his help. "I understand where we stand, and I'm not asking for anything but your carpentry skills." She paused and searched his eyes before adding, "I promise not to impose any expectations on you or Mattie Rose."

Aaron sighed as the lines around his eyes softened. "I can

help with the repairs, but we must keep things uncomplicated."

Lydia nodded, her heart aching with a bittersweet acknowledgment. "I agree. No need to open old wounds."

He gave her a reserved smile, a flicker of warmth breaking through the tense conversation. "Alright then. I can come after the store closes in the evening, and I'll need to bring Mattie Rose."

Gratitude flooded Lydia's face. "Thank you, Aaron. It means a lot to me."

***

As Lydia pulled away, her car's engine's gentle hum contrasting with the quiet countryside, Aaron stood there, his eyes fixed on her disappearing vehicle. The fading trail of dust stirred an array of emotions he fought hard to dismiss.

Closing his eyes, he took a deep-rooted breath, attempting to banish the longing that threatened to consume him. He clenched his fists, suffering the embedding pull of his heart and the rational voice in his head urging caution.

***

Lydia pushed open the heavy oak door and stepped into the quiet haven of the bookshop. Making her way upstairs, she picked up the small package Sami forwarded to her and removed it from its padded envelope. She examined the return postmark from Willow Springs as she opened it while settling into her father's easy chair. Once her hand hit the well-worn leather, her heart quickened as she fanned the pages. A small, heavy object slipped out between the pages and fell to her lap with a small thud. She gasped at her father's perfect penmanship.

Lydia carefully turned the pages, revealing a journey through his life over the last five years, beginning with the day she left him. Among the entries chronicling daily life, he left little messages for her. Tears welled in her eyes as she read about his yearning for her to return home. His tender words of missing her and the regret he held for wanting to rewrite the past laid heavy on her chest, leaving her gasping for air through the sobs.

For hours, she sat bathed in the sunlight, seeping through the upstairs apartment window and reading her father's journey through life without her in it. A few entries seemed out of place, particularly the page that outlined the value of his collection of first edition antique books locked in a glass case in the cellar. Another detailed his extensive research on the underground railroad that ran through downtown Willow Springs. Yet another spoke harshly about Harvey's desire to force him to sell the aging building. This prospect clashed with his dreams.

But then, in the very last entry on the day before he died, a warmth emerged within his words, his fervent wish for her to inherit the Book Cellar. A new sense of purpose ignited Lydia's eyes as she reread the entry. Her path suddenly became clear. She had to preserve the bookshop regardless of the challenge Harvey may present.

The ancient skeleton key on her lap was unlike anything she had ever seen, and it held a mystery only her father knew. The metal gleamed with a muted luster, hinting at a history concealed between its tarnished grooves. Puzzled, she turned the key in her hands, touching the weight and wondering what secrets it might unlock.

Dropping the key back inside the padded envelope, she discovered another folded letter that bore her father's words. The cryptic message, meant only for her, left her reeling in grief at her father's tender expressions. His passion for the written word shone in his beautiful words and gave her a comfort she hadn't felt in years.

Dearest Lydia,

There are no words I can say that can heal the deepest part of your hurting soul. The choices forced upon you were unbearable, and I hold no contempt toward you or what led to the bittersweet farewell you had to make to a piece of your heart.

We can put the distance between us to rest anytime you come home. There is no longer room in my life for judgment against my only daughter. The pages of your life are yours to pen, and I want you to know my unwavering love for you stands firm no matter what.

Should you yearn to reclaim what you lost, a path exists that will fill that void forever. Come home, Lydia; you hold the key to your future.

Datt

Lydia's hands trembled as she clutched the letter. The revelation that he knew about her long-lost child sent shivers down her spine, unleashing emotions she thought had been secretly tucked away. Confusion surrounded her as she descended the stairs to the bookshop.

With the key dangling from her fingers, she surveyed the store for any sign of a lock that might reveal the future her father spoke of. With her heart pounding, she inserted the key into every locked cabinet and door until all failed to release her father's promise.

***

Turning the 'Closed' sign, Lydia spoke kind words to the last customer as Aaron stood near the entrance with a toolbox. She greeted him with a hesitant smile. "Evening, Aaron."

He reacted with a nod, ushering Mattie Rose in through the door as her curious bluebird eyes darted between Lydia and the rows of neatly lined books.

Lydia couldn't help but notice his guarded look and the palpable distance that seemed to deepen since their last visit. "I appreciate you going out of your way to help me."

His eyes briefly met hers, his curt nod acknowledging his attitude. "I just wanted to finish what I started with your father."

Lydia swallowed hard at the mention of her father before replying, "I'll leave you to it then." She motioned Mattie Rose toward the kids' corner with everything a six-year-old would enjoy. "Let me know if you need anything," Lydia said, easing the somewhat flat atmosphere.

Lydia led Mattie Rose to the corner of the bookshop under the front windows. The sun added a subtle stream of light into the fading day as they sat on the floor.

With a gentle touch, Lydia picked up a copy of one of her favorite books and held it out for Mattie Rose, whose eyes lit up with the familiar gleam of recognition. "Would you like me to read it to you?"

Mattie Rose clutched the book and then focused on the glossy cover. Lydia smiled, the lines on her face softening with the little girl's fondness for the book she chose. "It's one of my favorites. I read it during story time every Saturday morning when I helped my *datt* with the store."

Though still silent, there was a tangible articulation on Mattie Rose's face as she turned the pages, and Lydia read over her shoulder. As they finished one and then another, the young girl accepted each book offered with an abundant nod, her eyes alight with curiosity about the story within.

"Sometimes, words in a story can say more than we ever can," Lydia muttered, watching Mattie Rose flip through the pages.

While Aaron worked on the repairs, he could not help but steal glances across the room at Lydia and Mattie Rose. A flicker of warmth tugged at the corner of his heart as he observed how Mattie Rose's eyes sparkled with joy as Lydia handed her a book. He had forgotten how much the child enjoyed books and had failed to indulge her in such things since Frannie passed away.

A pang of worry tightened Aaron's chest as he witnessed Mattie Rose warm up under Lydia's attention. His non-verbal and withdrawn daughter seemed to glow through the books Lydia offered. He suddenly feared what would happen if Mattie Rose got too close and Lydia left. The potential heartache the young girl would face again tore at his inner being.

Yet, amidst his reservations, other emotions stirred within him—a sense of gratitude. Lydia's gentle approach to Mattie Rose was hard to ignore. He resumed working through the repairs, stealing glances that betrayed the turmoil beneath the spot in his heart he thought had long forgotten Lydia Troyer.

Aaron moved the bookshelf he was repairing as Lydia walked beside him. "Thank you again. I was concerned about the stability of this shelf."

Aaron stood back and tucked his hammer back in his toolbelt. "I never noticed it before. I wonder how it got this way. Your father never pointed it out to me before."

Silence hung between them briefly before Aaron spoke again, his voice carrying a sliver of gratefulness. "Thanks for keeping Mattie Rose. I... I'd forgotten how much she enjoyed reading. Frannie used to read to her every day." He stopped, and she noticed the lines around his eyes tighten at his next confession. "I suppose I've been so concerned with her daily needs I've failed to..."

Lydia interrupted him. "Don't be so hard on yourself. It takes a lot to raise a child. You can't expect to remember everything she might need."

She noted the change in his demeanor, a slight thawing to his guarded exterior. "She's a joy to be around," Lydia replied, her voice gentle. "Books can bring people together, even without words."

A small smile touched Aaron's lips. "*Jah*, Frannie used to say just about the same thing. Seeing her smile today reminded me of those moments with Frannie. I appreciate that."

Lydia felt a warmth in her chest, a shared understanding.

"Anytime. If Mattie Rose enjoys books, we can make this a regular thing." She tilted closer and uttered, "Reading might be just what she needs to help her find her words again."

With a flicker of hope in his eyes, Aaron asked, "You think?"

Lydia nodded. "It didn't take her long to warm up to me. Perhaps she needs to open up to something different, a new way of expressing herself."

"I sure hope you're right. She starts school in two months, and I'm concerned."

Lydia glanced over at Mattie Rose, still sitting on the floor surrounded by books. In a hushed tone, she stated, "It's natural to worry, but I bet she's going to snap out of her silence as quick as she slipped into it. You watch and see."

***

Alone in the apartment, Lydia held her father's journal, it's weathered pages taunting her with the mystery it held. After taking a sip of herbal tea, she turned to the entry outlining each book's value in her father's downstairs collection. As a child, she couldn't examine the antique books without him being with her, and then only after they had gloved hands. The words on the pages ignited her curiosity like a spark in the darkness, and she headed downstairs. After retrieving the key to the locked glass case, she headed to the cellar.

The black abyss, a place she had known since childhood yet never fully explored, urged her on. The air grew denser as she ventured deeper into the back section of the unused space. With a flashlight in hand, she found the display case covered in dust. How she wished the electric lights the bishop approved for the bookshop included the cellar.

The eeriness of the night added to her apprehension. With gloved hands, she reached for a particularly weathered volume, and a strange sensation pricked at the back of her neck.

Faint whispers echoed through the walls. At first, she dismissed them as a figment of her imagination, the creaks and sighs of an old building playing tricks on her mind.

Yankee sat at her side. His fur bristled slightly, and Lydia couldn't help but notice the hair standing up on his back. A low growl rumbled intensely within his chest, a guttural sound that hinted at an awareness beyond her own.

But then the whispers grew into distinct voices. They rose and fell unsettlingly, forcing her to hold her breath and turn off the flashlight. A chill settled over her as the voices carried through the musty air. Fear crept in as the voices seemed trapped in the walls, holding her captive to the darkness. Yankee's stance reassured her, his loyalty a silent affirmation that she wasn't alone.

When the sounds faded, she summoned the courage to make her way out of the back room. Ascending the narrow staircase with the ancient book clutched tightly in her hands, the whispers from the cellar still lingered in her mind. As she reached the upstairs apartment, a sudden compulsion prompted her to lock the door behind her.

The dim kerosene lamp over the kitchen table cast an array of dancing shadows in the silence, adding a sense of uncertainty to the room. Alone in the apartment, an unrelenting fear gripped her heart, causing it to beat uncontrollably.

As she paced the room, her heightened imagination led her to second-guess her decision to stay in the apartment instead of Joshua and Melinda's.

Hoping to settle her nerves, she picked up the book she had retrieved from the case. As she opened it, a delicate map fell out, its edges worn and frayed. The map hinted at an underground railroad passage connected to the store, a revelation that made her study the map more closely.

The map lined up to the area of the cellar she was exploring and then weaved its way under Ruthie's bakery to the end of the street under the Mercantile, including the Sandwich Shoppe and the Restaurant on the Corner. The echoing voices in the cellar now seemed to find a home in the walls. As she studied the faded ink and carefully traced its path, she turned back to her father's journal.

As she compared the two, confusion settled over her brow. Her father's meticulous research, documented with care, spoke of the illegal use of the old tunnels and hiding spots along Main Street. The revelation left her wondering about the secrets her father had uncovered and why he felt he needed to pass them down to her.

Lydia traced her fingertip over her father's words. Questions danced in her mind, twirling like shadows from the lamp above her head. She held the old leather notebook close to her chest and whispered, "What are you trying to tell me, *Datt*? And why mail it to me?"

CHAPTER 6

S aturday morning dawned, leaving Lydia with mixed emotions as she prepared to open the bookshop on the last day of the week. The familiar creek of the wooden door announced the arrival of Ruthie, carrying a comforting offering of coffee and fresh from her oven cinnamon rolls.

"I figured you'd need an extra jolt this morning since it will most likely be a busy day for us both." Ruthie stated as she handed her a steaming mug.

Ruthie's kindness touched Lydia's heart, and the aroma of freshly brewed coffee settled her unease about the day. "I really don't know what to expect today." Lydia took a sip and broke off a piece of the gooey roll to sample before continuing. "I need to make sense of the orders and invoices on my *datt's* desk."

Just as the first customer came inside, Lydia's cell phone chimed. "Do you mind sticking around for a minute while I take this?" Ruthie agreed with a nod.

Lydia's screen displayed Ben Markle's name, and her stomach flipped as she swiped to answer her boss's call while walking to the back of the shop. "Hello."

"Lydia, It's Ben. I've been trying to reach you."

"Sorry, Mr. Markle. Things have been hectic," she responded in a tone with a balance of courtesy and reservation.

"I understand, but I need you back in Pittsburgh. Your position at Markle Media is crucial to our success, and we can't afford to be without you much longer. You're an integral part of the podcast team," he asserted with an urgency that left Lydia uneasy.

"I appreciate that, I really do. But right now, I need time to settle things here in Willow Springs, mainly with my father's bookshop."

There was a pause on the other end of the line before Mr. Markle spoke again, taking on a hint of persuasion. "What kind of things do you need to settle?"

Lydia hesitated, choosing her words carefully. "It's more about sorting out what my brothers want to do with things, and right now, I'm the only one free to keep things going to settle some of my father's debts."

There was a thoughtful pause on both ends before Mr. Markle spoke, "I understand your attachment to the bookshop, but I have people I can get on it to release you from the burden of the aging business. Let me sell it and handle the legalities so you can return to Pittsburgh."

His offer lingered in the air; his proposed involvement made her uneasy. "I appreciate the offer, but it's not just about the property; it was my father's life, and I can't just walk away from it right now."

Mr. Markle sweetened his manner. "Lydia, sometimes it's better to let go. The building is old, and real estate values in Willow Springs are only going up. Think about it. We could find a way to benefit, releasing you from the responsibility."

Something about how he knew about the buildings on Main Street and how he wanted to help seemed strangely personal, and she couldn't shake the feeling that there was more to his agenda than met the eye. "I have things under control," she declared. "If you could approve a short leave for me to take care of things, I'll try to get back as fast as I can. In the meantime, Sami is more than capable of taking over in my absence."

She heard him sigh before he said, "I'll give you a month. But remember, we're counting on you. Your job will be waiting, at least that long," he stated, his tone firm.

As she hung up the phone, suspicion clung to her thoughts. She couldn't shake the reaction he knew more about her situation than she alluded to. The conversation left her anxious about the timeline he imposed and the strange way he offered to help with things that had no bearing on him.

***

As the afternoon closed, Lydia grabbed Yankee's lead and ventured to the town park across from the bookshop. With looming thoughts of visiting Harvey and explaining her father's wishes for the bookshop swirling through her head, she hoped a walk would offer a respite from the uncertainties of life.

With Yankee trotting faithfully by her side, the warm summer day offered refuge in the simplicity of the moment.

Suddenly, the tranquility shattered as the roar of an engine sliced through the peaceful evening as her eyes darted toward the disturbance, and a breath caught in her throat. A red Camaro, much like the one her former *Englisch* boyfriend drove, emerged around the corner.

Fleeting memories surrounded her like an old, musty coat,

wrapping her with an unwelcome embrace. The car stopped within feet of where she stood on the sidewalk, and Yankee growled at her sudden unease. The car's intrusion brought an unexpected tension, and her pulse quickened as she braced herself for the encounter.

Jimmy Scott, handsome and still charming, greeted Lydia with a wry smile playing on his lips. "Well, if it isn't Lydia Troyer. I heard you had returned to Willow Springs."

Lydia gave Yankee an assuring pat as she asked, "What are you doing here, Jimmy?"

In a smug tone, he disclosed, "I'd say the same thing you are. Enjoying a peaceful summer evening."

Lydia gave him a wary glance. "No, I mean here—talking to me."

He turned the car off and stepped out, leaning casually against the car, scanning the buildings along Main Street. "Just passing through, thought I'd see how small-town life was suiting you," he replied, sending a chill down Lydia's spine.

"What do you want from me, Jimmy?"

"Now, now Lydia, don't get your feathers all out of sorts. I believe enough time has passed between us that we could have an adult conversation without any pretense of our past."

Lydia eyed Jimmy. "An adult conversation? You never gave me that courtesy before," her voice simmered with resentment.

He raised an eyebrow, the smug smile never leaving his face. "Water under the bridge."

She bit her lip, the wounds of the past still fresh beneath the surface. "Time may have passed, but some things are not easily forgotten."

Jimmy crossed his arms over his chest, and a few seconds lingered between them. "People can change."

She gave out a disgusted giggle. "I hardly believe that. Jimmy Scott doesn't change for anyone."

His jaw hardened for a moment, and he snapped. "Lydia, I didn't know what else to do. We were young, and I wasn't ready to be burdened with a child."

"Leaving me on the steps of that woman's center alone to make the hardest life decision is inexcusable."

Ignoring her statement, Jimmy's eyes lingered on the building that housed her father's bookshop, a sly grin on his lips. "Quite a place your old man had here."

Lydia's apprehension grew as she studied his expression. "What is it to you, Jimmy?"

"I have a keen interest in old buildings. Specifically since my father made me a partner in his real estate business." He shifted his feet and angled back on his car. "Old buildings like these on Main Street are prime locations for redevelopment plans, you know." He explained with a glint of unexplained interest.

Lydia's brow furrowed with a mix of anger and suspicion. "Redevelopment? What are you up to?" she demanded; her voice unwavering.

He chuckled in a low groan. "Lydia, Lydia, always the curious one. Let's just say I'm interested in the history of this town, especially the history tied to the buildings here on Main Street." He retorted, his words carrying the hint of a threat.

His implications hung in the air, and the knot in her stomach tightened as he reached over and kissed her cheek. She twisted from his reach, making him laugh and mutter, "There was a time when you didn't flinch at my touch. If I remember correctly, it didn't take me too long to break through those Old Order traditions you held close to."

All at once, she felt sick and could barely hold her stomach back from convulsing until he moved back inside his car. "I'll let you get settled in and perhaps I'll stop by and see you again," he claimed as he pulled away from the curb. Her insides shuddered with his declaration at his involvement in real estate, and his peculiar attentiveness to the history of the old buildings set off alarm bells in her mind.

***

As the apparent tension between Lydia and Jimmy unfolded, Aaron stood across the street as a silent observer. He didn't take his eyes off Lydia as a protective instinct surged through his veins as he noted her nervous body language and the unsettling effect Jimmy seemed to have on her.

He felt a pang of jealousy tugging at his emotions, a conflict to protect Lydia, and his hesitation at getting too close to her again. When the encounter finally ended, Aaron approached Lydia with a measured stride. "Everything okay?"

Her eyes darted nervously down the street as they watched his car disappear on South Main Street Extension. "He was asking questions about the bookshop and about the building." Turning toward him, she asked, "Have you seen him around Willow Springs much? "she inquired.

"It's hard not to miss that car. He tends to make his

existence known wherever he goes. He and his father have been trying to buy up all the businesses along Main Street."

"There's something off about all this, Aaron; I can feel it," she expressed, her unease evident.

"I think I've told you more than once he wasn't someone to be trusted." A worrisome silence hung between them, and Aaron sensed he may have just opened an old wound. "I'm sorry, that was uncalled for," he muttered.

"You have nothing to be sorry for. I should have listened to you five years ago," she countered.

As they stood on the quiet street, the shadows of the past hovered over Aaron as he wrestled with his emotions, torn between the desire to shield Lydia from the clutches of Jimmy Scott and the realization that their shared history may complicate matters more than he anticipated.

***

The tension between Harvey and Ed reached a boiling point in the dimly lit, cluttered dairy barn office. Stacks of disorganized paperwork and stale tobacco pouches left the air stagnant to the point of mirroring the escalating conflict.

"Ed, you've been stalling on finding that journal and the key to the bookcase for too long. How am I supposed to replace those old books if you've been unable to locate that journal?"

Ed leaned on an old rusty filing cabinet with a sneer on his face. "You should have kept your *schwester* away longer so I could have gotten back in there unnoticed."

Harvey clenched his jaw, a vein pulsing in his temple. "Like you did last time? I told you to leave things as you found them. The old man's journal holds the key to everything," Harvey snapped, his frustration evident.

He tipped back in his chair. "You're not working fast enough. How am I supposed to sell those old books without knowing which ones are valuable? Plus, other things in that journal need to disappear."

Ed slammed his fist on the desk, echoing through the small room. "I said I'm working on it. Keep pushing me, and you'll lose more than this farm."

Harvey leaned in, his voice dropping to a dangerous whisper. "Remember who you're talking to, boy! Time is something I don't have."

***

Lydia approached her *bruder's* office with caution. Voices muffled yet unmistakably angry bounced off the barn walls as she walked through the empty dairy barn. The Holstiens had already been milked and put out to pasture. When the argument intensified, Lydia treaded into the shadows just as Ed Glick departed.

Waiting a few seconds before moving to the open door, she took a deep breath and pulled her shoulders back as she moved into the doorway. "Harvey?" she called tentatively.

Harvey's head snapped up from the stack of papers. "What do you want?" His words teemed with irritation. "Can't you see I'm busy?"

Lydia swallowed hard. "I just wanted to talk to you about the bookshop."

"Why did you come back, Lydia?" Harvey groaned, exasperated, running his hand through his long beard. "I have enough on my plate. The last thing I needed was to deal with you."

Lydia squared her shoulders again. "If I hadn't come, who would be here to see that the store opened back up?"

"I couldn't care less if it ever opened back up. We need to sell it and be done with it. All it does is cost us money. Who do you think has funded most of the maintenance all these years?"

Lydia furrowed her eyebrows in confusion. "I suspected it was profitable enough to support itself. Are you telling me it hasn't been?" She took another breath, trying to remain calm despite the rising tension between her and Harvey.

Harvey shook his head. "I've been trying to talk *Datt* into selling it for years. The money could be used elsewhere throughout this family."

Lydia frowned, unable to comprehend why Harvey wanted to sell something that meant so much to their father and family history. "*Datt* didn't want to sell the store, he wanted to…"

Harvey interrupted her. "I couldn't care less what he wanted to do. As soon as I can get things squared away, we will sell it."

Lydia picked up her father's book about the underground railroad off Harvey's desk. "Do you know that *Datt* believed there to be railroad passageways under the store and others on Main Street?"

"Hogwash! Just old tales that have never been proved, and I told the old man as much."

"But don't you see? If we can prove there's truth to his claims, we could breathe new life into Willow Springs. People would come from all over to learn about the underground railroad and our town's role in it," she argued passionately.

Harvey let out an annoyed grunt. "I don't have time for your fanciful ideas, Lydia. I've got real problems just trying to keep this farm afloat."

Lydia's heart sank as she realized Harvey wouldn't be open to anything she had to say, especially finding their father's true wishes for the bookshop in his journal. As she turned to leave, Harvey asked, "Do you remember anything about that old book collection *Datt* had?"

"Not really. Why?"

Harvey's countenance darkened. "Just curious. How about his journal? It seems to have come up missing, and I need to find it."

Lydia's heart skipped a beat, her mind racing as she tried to devise a believable response. "I... I didn't find it in his things."

His jaw clenched, his frustration evident in her reply. "Well, you'd better not be hiding anything from me. That journal is important, and I need to find it," he warned, his mood leaving a trail of suspicion behind.

She nodded, her stomach churning with guilt. "I'll keep an eye out for it," her words were cluttered with lies.

As she turned to leave, Lydia couldn't shake the

overwhelming sensation of unease. Despite Harvey's harsh treatment, she vowed to live out her father's true intentions and uncover the truth between the walls of the cellar. A strange thought entered her mind when she wondered why Harvey had her father's book about the railroad on his desk. Didn't Aaron mention they'd been looking at it just before he passed away?

As Lydia strode back into the sunlight, she was startled to see Ed leaning casually against her car, a sly grin on his face, with a toothpick balanced between his teeth which he promptly pulled out to spit tobacco on the ground. The hairs on her neck set off an alarm, and she approached cautiously.

"Ed, what are you doing here?"

He straightened up, his eye lingering on her with an unsettling force. "Just thought I'd catch up with you darlin'," he smirked.

"I'm not anyone's darlin' and get away from my car."

"Oh…I see city life left you a bit brassy," he snarled.

Lydia's stomach churned as she cringed back, instinctively putting some distance between them. "What do you want?"

Ed's grin widened. "Just thought we could have a little chat and see if there was anything of our past we could salvage now that you're back in Willow Springs."

"Our past? I don't remember us having anything other than my annoyance at your creepy behavior."

Ed's smile faded before he regained his composure, his eyes narrowing at her comment. "So, I was nothing but a creep to you?" he asked, his tone casual but insulted.

Lydia tried to push past him to get into her car, but he grabbed her arm and hissed in her ear. "You've seen nothing of how unnerving I can be, darlin'."

She pulled away from his grasp. "You don't scare me, Ed Glick."

He dropped her arm and shrugged, his grin forming a smirk. "Well, you best think twice about that. I know too much and can use what I know at the drop of a hat to get what I want."

Lydia eyed him suspiciously, her instincts screaming for her to tread lightly. "What business do you have with Harvey?"

In a smug attitude, he replied, "Let's just say I'm doing a little research. Gathering some information."

Lydia crawled into her car, and as Ed sauntered away, she knew it wasn't the last encounter she'd have with him. Something about him lurking beneath the surface left her unsettled, and she couldn't shake the nagging sense that his intentions were far from innocent.

As Lydia steered her car around the back of the barn, she couldn't help but spot Harvey standing at the window, his disdainful glare burning through the car windshield. His cold expression displayed an aura of resentment. Her heart sank as she realized the depth of his animosity towards her. It was a bitter pill to swallow, and she wondered if she'd ever be able to break through his will enough for him to accept her back into his life.

With a heavy sigh, she pulled back out onto Spring Quarry Road, and a flicker of defiance ignited within her, fueling a new determination to prove her worth and reclaim her rightful place in the Troyer family.

CHAPTER 7

Lydia busied herself behind the bookshop counter, her mind buzzing about the map she found in one of her father's antique books. She wanted to return to the cellar and look through the case of old books again, but the night's strange noises kept her locked up tightly in her apartment.

The hum of conversation from a few customers mulling around faded in the background as she pored over the old map. She had pulled every book she had on the underground railroad that ran through Pennsylvania and compared her notes to the few her father had outlined in his journal.

A twinge of guilt hovered over her at lying to Harvey, but until she discovered the truth, she was determined to keep her secret.

When Aaron arrived early to start back at the repairs, she greeted him with a sense of urgency, her excitement barely contained as she motioned over to the counter. "You won't believe what I found. Look at this."

"What's this?" he asked, his brow furrowing with curiosity.

Lydia pointed to the faded lines on the map, tracing the path of the rail passages that would lay beneath the streets of Willow Springs. "This is it," she explained, her voice held at a whisper. "The passage that runs under our feet. Can you imagine this building playing a big part in freeing slaves?"

"Where did you get this?" He asked as he studied the map, turning it so it lined up with the contour of the store and street. "So, your father was correct in his research?" he continued to ask in a hushed tone.

"I think *Datt* was on to something, and if we can prove it true, this could be a big boost for Willow Springs and the historical society. All the buildings on Main Street would be affected and their value would increase substantially."

"That sheds some light on Jimmy's sudden concern in the buildings on Main Street," he pronounced.

"Oh… my! You're right. Aaron, I forgot to tell you I heard voices in the cellar last week, and there have been strange things happening in the store I can't explain."

Aaron's voice took on a protective edge. "Strange things like what?"

"Little things out of place, and I can't shake the impression that someone's been tampering with my things, plus noises I can't explain. Even Yankee seems nervous and barks at every little thing all night long. I even double-checked all the locks, and everything was secure." She shook her head and wiped her hand across her forehead. "Most likely, it's all in my head."

"I doubt that. Maybe it would be better to stay at Joshua's at night," Aaron declared, his voice laced with concern.

"And then there's Harvey," Lydia explained, "he's been asking about *Datt's* journal and seems awfully interested in his antique books." She paused and tilted in closer. "I lied to him. I told him I knew nothing of the books or where *Datt's* journal is."

"What's so important about that?" he asked.

Lydia stooped, pulled the leather-lined notebook from her bag, and flipped through the pages until she found the one that outlined each book's value in his collection. Then she turned to the page where he outlined his plans for the store. As Aaron read over her shoulder, he commented with a long sigh, "Oh, this changes everything. Do you think Harvey knows he left the store to you?"

Before Lydia could respond, Detective Powers entered the

bookshop, the look on his face commanding their attention.

"Lydia, Aaron," Detective Powers greeted them solemnly. "I have some news about your father's death."

Lydia held up a finger instructing him to wait until she checked out a lingering customer and turned the open sign before making her way back to the counter.

"The lab results from your father's pipe came back, and it appears that he was indeed poisoned."

Lydia pulled a hand to her chest and gasped. "Poisoned?" she echoed, her voice barely above a whisper.

The detective nodded. "Yes. It seems someone tampered with his pipe tobacco, lacing it with a lethal dose of rat poison."

Lydia couldn't speak, the shock evident on her face, and Aaron asked, "Who would want to harm Wally?"

Detective Powers sighed. "That's what we need to figure out. But it's clear someone had a motive to silence him."

Lydia's mind raced with the possibilities as she struggled to understand what the detective presented. Could Harvey be involved somehow? Or was there someone else who might have learned of her father's discovery and what it could mean to the merchants on Main Street? Without saying a word, she pulled on Aaron's shirt sleeve and pointed to the map.

"Lydia found this map in the cellar," Aaron explained. "It outlines the route of the underground railroad that runs beneath the streets of Willow Springs."

Detective Powers studied the map. "If your father was onto something, it could have put him in danger. Word has it, there are certain people who have been strong-arming some of the Main Street merchants into selling their buildings. If my suspicions are correct, someone out there knows the value of these buildings and is trying to snatch them up before word gets out about the history associated with them."

Finally, Lydia calmed her racing heart enough to ask, "But to go as far as killing him? Who would do such a thing?"

The detective's face softened as he tried to explain the true intent of criminals. "You have no idea what people will do for the love of money."

***

A quiet lull in the afternoon brought Lydia a much-earned break from the steady stream of customers that had occupied her time all morning. Aaron finished up with one of his other jobs and stopped in to put another layer of mud on the new drywall in the store's bathroom. Lydia didn't notice anything but Aaron's comforting hum as he worked, and the sounds of footsteps approaching the counter caught her attention. She glanced up to see Ben Markle standing before her. His polished appearance and confident demeanor made a statement long before she greeted him.

"Mr. Markle, what brings you here?"

"Lydia, my dear, how lovely to see you. I had business in the area and wanted to stop in and see if I could convince you to come back to work early."

He strolled closer, eyes sweeping over the bookshop with a faint interest. "It's such a shame to see such a historical establishment facing uncertain times." He exclaimed, his voice smooth and practiced.

"What do you mean uncertain times?" Lydia asked cautiously.

Ben flashed her a charming smile. "It's no secret Willow Springs has seen better days, and by the looks of this building, it's showing signs of serious wear." He waited to look around again before continuing, "And with your father gone, I can only imagine the burden it must be for you and your family to keep things afloat financially."

Like a lightning bolt, Detective Powers' warning about people wanting to snatch up the real estate along Main Street set alarms off in Lydia's mind, and she couldn't help but state, "We're handling things just fine, thank you."

His smile extended across his face as he expressed, "I meant nothing by it other than perhaps it's time to consider other options. I could make you a generous offer for the property." He leaned across the counter and breathed in a husky voice. "With the proceeds, you could return to work sooner. Think of the opportunities it could afford you."

Lydia's mind raced with conflicting emotions as she considered his proposal. On the one hand, the prospect of financial security and a successful career was tempting. But on the other hand, something about his offer didn't sit right with her, particularly after what she learned from Detective Powers. She couldn't help but feel uncomfortable and shifted uneasily under his intense stare.

"Lydia, you have so much potential. You could go far in the company with your talent and work ethic. Imagine all the opportunities that await you back in the city."

Her cheeks flushed with embarrassment as his words washed over her, but more so, she felt ashamed of his behavior with Aaron within earshot of their conversation. "I... I appreciate your concern for my well-being, but I'm not sure when or if I'll ever return to Pittsburgh."

The intense glint in his eyes made Lydia's skin crawl. "Come now, Lydia," his tone was serious as he moved around the counter. "You're too talented to waste away in this backward town." He laid his hand over hers. "With me, you could have more than you could ever dream of having."

She freed her hand and backed away from him, stumbling over the stool only to catch herself before falling to the ground. The noise alerted Aaron, and she instantly saw him over Mr. Markle's shoulder. "Please," she said firmly, her voice trembling with emotion. "This is inappropriate, and I won't stand for what you're insinuating." After getting her footing, she stated, "I'm no longer interested in working for you. I have a business to run, and that's where my focus needs to be... right here in Willow Springs."

When Aaron stepped closer, Mr. Markle moved back and lifted his hands in defense. "You're making a mistake. Don't go rushing into anything. Your emotions are still running high. I'll stop by and see you again and perhaps you will have come to your senses."

As he turned on his heel and strode out of the bookshop, Lydia let out a shaky breath, her hands trembling with relief as Aaron moved beside her. "Are you okay?" he asked.

"*Jah*, I'm sorry you had to witness that." Overwhelmed by Mr. Markle's unwanted advances and the uncertainty of the bookshop, Lydia felt a wave of embarrassment come over her. She felt Aaron towering close, and without hesitation, she buried her face in her hands, and he pulled her close into his chest. She soaked in the familiar scent of hard work and fresh air, finding a fleeting moment of comfort in his quick embrace.

Aaron's voice was a gentle breath against her ear. "I can't bear the thought of you returning to work for a man who would treat you this way."

Tucked safely in Aaron's arms, Lydia felt a small glimmer of hope flicker to life. She knew she made the right decision to stay in Willow Springs and confront the challenges with the bookshop.

Before she could thank Aaron for his vote of confidence, he pulled away. "I need to finish and pick up Mattie Rose from Melinda's." His quick departure left her wondering if she had misread his support and made her wish she hadn't collapsed in his arms.

***

Lydia's sweet scent stayed with Aaron long after he left the bookshop. All the way to pick up Mattie Rose, he couldn't get her face from his mind and the way Markle used his sleazy persuasion to offer her things no God-fearing woman would agree to. The way he spoke to her made him sick to his stomach, and an overwhelming need to protect her from the *Englisch* businessman tugged at his conscience.

When he arrived, Mattie Rose was waiting by the door, her small frame eager for his arrival. After waving at Melinda, he lifted Mattie Rose into the buggy, noticing the book Lydia gave her last week clutched tightly in her hands. As he pulled out of the driveway, she kept pointing to the book, her eyes pleading as she tried to convey her wish to go to the bookshop.

Frustration gnawed at Aaron as he tried to understand her silent gestures. "Look, Mattie Rose, you need to use your words; I'm not a mind reader," he urged with a twinge of exasperation. "What do you want? I'm not doing anything until you find a way to get that tongue of yours working again."

But Mattie Rose remained silent, her lips pressed in tight lines as tears pooled on her eyelashes as she persisted to point at the book. Aaron shook his head, keeping his eyes on the road and snapping the reins to bring the horse to a comfortable trot.

There was only rustling wind through the open buggy, along with the horse's hooves on the blacktop for a few moments. And then, to Aaron's amazement, Mattie Rose spoke, her voice soft and hesitant.

"L-Lydia," she muttered, her eyes closed as she uttered the name.

Lydia's name on his daughter's lips sounded like heaven, but he refused to make a big deal of his surprise. "Lydia?" he repeated, "You want to see Lydia?"

Mattie Rose nodded, a small smile tugging at the corner of her mouth as she looked up at him with pleading eyes.

He wasn't sure who was more pleased to be going back to Lydia's, Mattie Rose or himself. Without another word, he drove past his driveway and back into town, his mind consumed with the unexpected turn of events keeping her in their lives.

***

A knock on the door startled them both, and Yankee's bark covered the small apartment. Lydia hurried to the window, her heart jumping as she saw Aaron and Mattie Rose standing at the bookshop door.

Opening the door, she greeted them warmly, overjoyed with the unexpected visitors. "Aaron, Mattie Rose, what a pleasant surprise."

Aaron offered an apologetic smile. "I hope we're not intruding. Mattie Rose insisted on coming to get a new book, and, well, I couldn't resist after she voiced her wishes herself."

Lydia gave him a surprised look as she turned her attention to Mattie Rose. "Not at all. I'm overjoyed that Mattie Rose is ready for a new book already."

They all walked to the kids' corner, and Lydia handed Mattie Rose the next book in the series they'd been enjoying. "I was just starting to think about supper. Can I entice the two of you to stay for roasted chicken and macaroni and cheese?"

Mattie Rose looked up at Aaron, her eyes pleading for an acceptable answer as Aaron replied, "Macaroni and cheese is one of her favorites, not sure how I can turn down such a tempting invitation."

Lydia led them up the stairs into her apartment, and as she busied herself in the kitchen, Aaron knelt beside Mattie Rose. "What is this book about?"

Mattie Rose beamed at her father, clutching the book tightly to her chest. "Family." She said, her voice soft yet overflowing with excitement.

Lydia turned from the kitchen, her eyes shining with delight. "Did she just say family? Oh, that's wonderful, Mattie Rose!" she claimed, unable to contain her excitement.

Aaron's eyes filled with pride. "Two words in one day. I'd say that's a miracle!"

As they all sat down for supper, conversation flowed between them. A new excitement saturated the air as they let go of the past for a few hours to enjoy Mattie Rose's new breakthrough. Aaron and Lydia discussed the hidden tunnels and their potential connection to the strange occurrences Lydia had experienced recently.

"I can't shake the feeling that the passageway might explain how someone got into the store with the doors locked," Aaron mused in intense thought.

Lydia nodded in agreement. "It's certainly a possibility. I've been too nervous about going down there again by myself." She paused, waiting for Mattie Rose to play with Yankee in the other room. "Do you mind exploring it further? Perhaps we can find a clue that proves *Datt's* theory?"

After they settled Mattie Rose down with her new book and left Yankee to keep her company, Lydia and Aaron made their way to the darkest back corners of the cellar. With the dim light of the flashlight casting eerie shadows on the walls, they combed through the clutter, searching for any sign of the hidden passageway, but their efforts proved fruitless.

As they emerged from the cellar, Lydia couldn't help but voice her disappointment. "Well, it looks like *Datt* may have been wrong. Or at least misguided in thinking this building was connected to secret tunnels."

Aaron replied, "I'm not ready to give up so fast. I think we need to look again but with better light. I have a couple of battery-operated construction lights at the house. I'll bring them next time, and we'll look again." He followed her up the stairs and resumed. "For as much as your *datt* loved history and research, I find it hard to believe he would be wrong about such an important fact about Willow Springs."

Lydia spread the map of Willow Springs and the surrounding area on the table, surrounded by the stack of books she had gathered. Aaron bowed in, studying the map's details as he listened to Lydia's explanations.

"Did I tell you I saw that book *In Hot Pursuit* on Harvey's desk?"

Aaron looked at her, the crease in his forehead taking on a defined line. "Now that's strange. I suppose he could also own a copy, but I find it odd that your father's copy is missing."

Lydia's mind raced with an unsettling possibility that Harvey, her own *bruder*, could have been involved in their father's death. "I can't believe I'm even considering this," she muttered, her voice trembling with disbelief. "But the more I think about it, the more it seems like Harvey might have had a motive."

Aaron nodded grimly. "It's hard to ignore the facts, Lydia. Why is he so interested in the journal and the book collection? But more than anything else, why and how did he end up with your father's book? Harvey must have been in the store right before he passed away. If so, why?"

Their conversation was interrupted by a loud crash, followed by Yankee barking furiously. Lydia's heart leaped into her throat as Aaron took off downstairs.

Mattie Rose ran to Lydia's side and buried her head in her side. "It's okay, I'm sure something just fell over." As she held tightly to the small girl, the possibility that Harvey could be capable of murder hung over her like a dark cloud, casting a shadow of doubt on everything she knew about her *bruder*.

Lydia's heart pounded with adrenaline as she listened to Aaron's account of what he found in the cellar. The thought of a crate of books crashing down on the glass display case of old books left Lydia shaken.

"A blast of cold air?" Lydia repeated, her voice shaking with concern. "That's strange. There shouldn't be any drafts down there."

Aaron grunted a troubled sound. "Exactly. I checked the windows and doors, but everything was still locked up tight. It's like the cold came from somewhere else."

Yankee interrupted their conversation with frantic barking. Lydia exchanged a worried look with Aaron as he took off back downstairs, calling the lab with him as he left.

They made their way back down into the cellar with cautious steps, bracing themselves for whatever mystery awaited them in the darkness.

CHAPTER 8

Carefully sifting through the old books salvaged from the shattered glass case, Lydia's fingers brushed against something unexpected tucked between the pages of one of the old books.

"What have you found?" Aaron asked, his voice tinged with curiosity.

Lydia held up the yellowed newspaper article, her eyes scanning the faded print. "It's an article about the black market using underground passages for their operations," she explained. "And look at these notes *Datt* made."

Aaron moved to read over her shoulder. "This is serious," he murmured. "If the black market has moved into Willow Springs, we must tread carefully." He paused to read more of the article before adding, "We need to show this to Detective Powers. This adds a new level to why people are trying to buy up these old buildings."

As they dug deeper into the books, the weight of their discoveries bore down on Lydia, leaving her overwhelmed with its severity. Fear rose as she re-read the article and her father's handwritten notes along the margin. "It was like my father kept a whole other world hidden beneath the surface." She sighed, brushing her hair away from her face with the back of her hand. "Who else knows about this, and what do we do now?" she asked Aaron.

"We can't rush into anything," Aaron advised. "Let's give the detective time to investigate what your father has detailed. We don't want to tip off whoever is behind all this, especially if this had anything to do with your father's death."

"I think I need to go to Joshua about this," Lydia said.

"*Nee*, not yet. This is bigger than any of us, and if we let word out about any of it, the bishop will step in and force us to keep it to ourselves. He will not look favorably on us going to Detective Powers, and surely the leaders will quiet us to keep peace in the community."

Lydia sat up straight in her chair. "They can quiet you, but not me. I'm not a member of the church." She glanced at Aaron with worried eyes. "I shouldn't have involved you in any of this."

"Don't worry about me," he said, his voice filled with conviction. "And as for involving me, don't think twice about it. I chose to be here."

Lydia's tense shoulders relaxed under Aaron's words as she called Detective Powers.

***

The detective sat at his desk and sifted through the paperwork, trying to make sense of the anonymous tip he had received earlier that day. The tip pointed to suspicious activities in the area, especially implicating Ed Glick, a member of the local Amish community, in unlawful dealings related to the black-market activities his department was investigating.

He needed an inside source to the Old Order community to help him gather more information from a group of people who did all they could to not involve outside sources. The atmosphere was tense as he debated what to do next to stop the illegal activity infiltrating his small town.

Suddenly, his cell phone rang, breaking the silence. He glanced at the caller ID and saw it was Lydia Troyer.

"Lydia, what can I do for you?" Lewis's voice was touched

with curiosity.

Lydia clicked her phone so Aaron could hear their conversation. "Aaron is here with me, and I have you on speaker. We came across some things in my father's books that you might find of importance. It seems he was following some black-market activity throughout Willow Springs."

Lewis exhaled. "Well, isn't that interesting? I received some anonymous tips today about the very same thing. It seems there's been some chatter about Ed Glick's involvement in the underground railroad passageways and possibly the black market."

"Goodness," Lydia exclaimed. "I wouldn't put it past him for sure and certain."

"Why do you say that, Lydia?"

"Nothing that I can prove. It's just a suspicion I have about him."

Detective Powers' chair squeaked as he shifted before saying, "Aaron, if these tips are to be believed, Ed may be involved in smuggling goods through the underground passages. I need your help to gather more information and possibly shed some light on what's happening."

Lydia quickly stated. "Ed was out at my brother Harvey's

the other day, and even though I hate to admit Harvey might be involved, I must admit he's been acting quite strange about things involving my father and the bookshop." Lydia paused and chewed her bottom lip.

"What do you think they might have in common, Lydia?"

"I have no idea, and I found it odd that Ed was even there. They were having some sort of argument, but I couldn't hear what they were saying. And then there's the fact that Harvey had my father's book about the underground railroad, which seems suspicious."

"I see. That does raise some red flags. We'll need to consider the possibility that your brother may also be involved. Do you have any other reasons to suspect him?"

Lydia hesitated and looked at Aaron to offer some comfort before continuing. "He has been hinting that he wants to sell this building. I can't help but wonder if he has ulterior motives, exclusively with his connection to Ed."

Aaron asked, "What can we do to help?"

The chair creaked again, and Lewis answered in a serious tone. "I need you both to watch Harvey and Ed Glick. Watch their movements, who they talk to, and anything suspicious. We need to gather as much information as possible to build a case.

And I can't do that when the Amish community clams up as tight as a tin can when I'm around."

Lydia exhaled. "It'll be easier for Aaron than myself, but I'll do what I can with keeping an eye on Harvey. Ed works at the Sandwich Shoppe, and I go there often, so I can keep on eye him."

"Just blend in, act naturally. You both know the Amish community. Use that to your advantage. But be discreet. We don't want them to catch on that they're being watched."

Aaron gave Lydia a worrisome glance and asked Lewis. "And what should we do if we see something suspicious?"

"Take notes," Detective Powers answered firmly. "Document everything you see, no matter how insignificant it may seem. We'll review your findings and see if we can determine what he's up to."

Lydia waited until the detective finished explaining how he wanted to handle things before she asked, "Any more news on my *datt's* pipe and tobacco?"

"Yes, Lydia. I've been tracing the source of the poisoned tobacco. It appears that the brand is sold in several convenience stores around town. However, the key factor here is who had access to your father's tobacco pouch."

"So, it could have been anyone who knew *Datt* smoked that brand? And what about the poison?"

Detective Powers groaned. "Again, we live in a farming community, and rat poison is readily available. Both are proving to be a dead end, and I'm not sure how much time the chief will allow me to spend on it since we have no autopsy report to create a tight case."

Aaron leaned in closer to the phone Lydia still held out. "If it's a matter of who had access, almost everyone knew he'd go outside to smoke his pipe throughout the day. Anyone could have gone through the cellar to the back porch."

"Exactly!" Detective Powers admitted. "It's crucial we narrow down the list of suspects based on who had knowledge of that. If either of you remember anything unusual or anyone who might have a reason to want to silence your father, please let me know."

"We'll keep that in mind. Thank you for the update." Lydia shut the phone and turned back toward Aaron.

***

Aaron lightened his steps as he heard muffled voices as he

turned the corner after leaving the bookshop. Stopping and observing Ed Glick from the shadows of Main Street, Aaron surveyed and listened with care. The sight of a bike parked beside Ed raised more questions than answers. Amish tradition in Willow Springs forbade the use of bicycles, making the detail particularly curious. Could Ed be going against the *Ordnung*?

Aaron stayed hidden, his eyes trying to adjust to the darkness as he observed Ed talking to the person in the sleek black car. There was tension in the air, and Aaron's instincts told him something was amiss. The corner streetlight cast shadows over Ed, and Aaron strained to catch snippets of their conversation, but the distance made it impossible to hear.

As Ed reached for his backpack, Aaron's pulse quickened. What could he be pulling out? He struggled to make out what the small item was. When Ed passed it through the window, a flicker of light fell on a book. Aaron sucked in a silent breath and held it, knowing he needed to gather as much information as possible without revealing himself. Silently, he made mental notes of everything he saw, committing the details to memory.

Aaron's suspicion deepened as Ed pulled the book from his bag and exchanged it with the person in the car. The transaction was swift, but the exchange of money was unmistakable. Once

Ed and the vehicle departed, Aaron slipped out of the shadows and returned to the bookshop.

Lydia had already turned off all the lights when he knocked on the front door. The sound of her feet descending the stairs gave Aaron time to look around the barren street for any other signs he should note. When the door opened, he pushed himself inside. "Lydia, I saw Ed and witnessed him exchange a book with a man in the black car for money."

Lydia looked up, concern on her face. "What do you mean?"

"He pulled a book from his backpack and exchanged it for money." His words tumbled out. "It didn't look right."

Lydia rubbed her arms with her hands and whispered, "I don't like it one bit." Suddenly, she took off running up the stairs. "Oh...my...why didn't I think of this before?" He followed her up the stairs as she continued, "*Datt's* book collection! Why didn't we compare the list in the journal to the books we pulled from the case?"

They compared the list to the books across the table for the next thirty minutes, and sure enough, one of the titles was missing.

Lydia sighed in disbelief. "We can't ignore this. We need to share this with Detective Powers. I think it's important.

If *Datt* felt it necessary to include a detailed record of each book and then send me the journal, it was an important fact he wanted me to know."

***

The very next day, Detective Powers showed up at the bookshop to examine the collection. He studied each book cautiously and even put on white gloves as Lydia required. "These books might be crucial to the case," he remarked, flipping through the pages of some of the weathered volumes.

Lydia's growing concern mounted with each passing minute. "I'm glad you're taking it seriously, especially after what Aaron witnessed last night."

Detective Powers glanced over at her. "I'd like to bring in an antiquarian. I've contacted someone I know in Erie who is on his way to look over your father's collection. He should be here anytime now."

Lydia hesitated for a moment before nodding. "Yes, of course, if you think it will help to know more about them."

"If my hunch is correct, I think some of these books are fakes."

Alarmed at the detective's suggestion, Lydia picked a volume up and examined it more carefully. "I know a lot about books but not as much as my father did. But I find it hard to believe my father wouldn't know a fake if he saw it."

"That's just it. By how he has each volume cataloged, I'm sure he had the original at one point."

Lydia's heart sank with the news, and she asked, "So, do you think someone switched some of these books out with fake ones?"

"It's certainly a possibility. First edition books like this could go for a pretty penny at an antique book sale."

A few minutes later, the book specialist arrived, carefully examining each book with a practiced eye. After a thorough inspection, he shook his head. "I'm afraid to say, but some of these books are replicas. Good ones if I say so myself, but definitely reproductions," he announced, disappointment evident in his voice. "They hold no significant value. However, these other books are quite valuable." He held up one of the oldest books and smiled. "I'd be willing to pay you triple what's listed in your father's journal for this volume."

"Oh, I couldn't part with them. They meant so much to my father. But if I ever decide to sell, I'll keep your contact information."

***

As Aaron's brown-topped buggy trotted along the familiar road into town, he glanced at Mattie Rose, who was tying her black *kapp* strings under her chin and swinging her tiny feet off the bench seat. The rhythmic clip-clop of horse hooves echoed off the blacktop and added to the warm afternoon setting.

"Mattie…I was thinking about Lydia."

Just at the mention of Lydia's name, Mattie's face took on a new level of brightness. Curious, her eyes turned to him, but she didn't utter a word, just smiled.

He couldn't help but smile back at her bright blue eyes looking back at him tenderly. "You like Lydia and Yankee, *jah*?"

Her little head bobbed eagerly. Aaron chuckled softly, his heart warming at the mention of Lydia's name. "Me too, and I think it would be nice for us to spend a little more time together." Mattie Rose beamed with delight; her evident enthusiasm infectious. "How about we stop and pick up lunch and surprise her with a picnic?"

As they resumed their slow journey into town, he couldn't help but feel a sense of anticipation building within him. The prospect of spending more time with Lydia and the drama surrounding her father's death filled him with excitement—he only prayed she would want the same.

With the heavy door creaking open, Lydia looked up from behind the bookshop counter to see Aaron and Mattie Rose walking in, their faces lit up with excitement. She couldn't help but smile at the sight of them, her apprehension momently forgotten with the warmth of the presence.

"Picnic?" Mattie Rose exclaimed, her eyes glimmering with excitement.

"Are you and your *datt* going on a picnic? That sounds lovely. Where are you going?" Lydia couldn't help but notice the little girl's lips turn up as she looked up at her father.

"We...ahh...hoped you'd join us," Aaron said. "I thought you could use a change of scenery, and it would be nice to spend some time outside of the bookshop," he explained, his voice warm and inviting.

"Are you sure? I didn't think..."

Aaron interrupted her. "It's just a friendly picnic."

Lydia nodded, her heart taking on a new pace. She couldn't deny her growing connection to Aaron and Mattie Rose. But she couldn't help but wonder if it was a mistake getting too close to him. If she let herself get involved with him, she'd be forced to tell him the one secret about her past she held tightly under lock and key. "Thank you for inviting me," Lydia said, even with the uncertainty gnawing at her insides. But when she looked into Aaron's eyes, she saw nothing but sincerity in his invitation.

CHAPTER 9

Jimmy carried a stack of folders into his father's office and waited until he looked up from his laptop. His father, the owner of Scott Properties, had a stern look etched on his face and studied him with a critical eye before pointing to the chair opposite his desk.

"You'd better have good news to report about those buildings in Willow Springs. This deal with Ben Markle could mean a game changer for our company."

"I'm working on it," Jimmy responded, trying to sound as confident as he could without stretching the truth. "I'm planning on visiting Lydia Troyer this morning. Perhaps I can convince her to sell so she can return to her life in Pittsburgh. I'm almost certain she's had enough of Willow Springs. I can't imagine she wants to stay much longer."

His father sat back in his chair, tapping his thumbs on its arms. "I'd thought you'd have this tied up by now. Use that

Scott charm I gave you and convince her any way you can… no matter the cost.

Some of the other partners think I should put someone else on this project. They feel you don't have enough experience, and I've heard rumors that you've maintained a history with the girl." He stopped, waiting for Jimmy to respond. "Is there any truth to that? If I remember correctly, I warned you about getting too emotionally involved with the girl, especially since she was a valuable part of our overall plan for Willow Springs."

Jimmy struggled to keep his composure at the mention of Lydia's name. "At one time… but nothing that would affect our plans for the Main Street project." Jimmy swallowed hard before continuing. "And there's nothing left of that now that would stand in our way."

In a demanding pitch, his father replied, "I hope you understand the importance of maintaining our reputation, Jimmy. We can't afford any scandals or distractions."

Jimmy clenched his fingers around the folders on his lap. "I would never do anything to jeopardize my position here."

With a dismissive nod, his father answered, "Good. Because if I were to find out you have, there will be consequences."

***

Jimmy sat in his car parked across from the bookshop, his eyes fixed on the entrance as he examined Lydia speaking with two men just outside the door, her stance stern and serious.

Sensing the opportunity to catch Lydia before opening the store, he approached with determined strides. "Lydia."

She turned to his voice, the look on her face guarded as she sized him up. "What are you doing here?"

"Wasn't that Detective Powers? Is everything alright?"

"We were just discussing some business matter. Nothing that concerns you."

As she turned to step back into the store, Jimmy followed her, saying, "You know, Lydia, I've been thinking a lot about our past. About what we once had."

Stopping in her tracks, she turned and gave him the curtest glance. "And what exactly are you getting at?"

Jimmy smirked. "Just that maybe there's still something there between us." He stepped closer. "Something worth exploring."

Lydia's eyes took on a stubborn stare as she moved back. "I have no interest in revisiting whatever we had in the past. Do you understand me?"

"Come on, Lydia. Don't be like that." Jimmy snorted an evil laugh before adding, "You know I've always had a way of getting what I want."

Lydia held the door open for him to leave. "Not this time. You can't manipulate me anymore."

He stood still, not ready to leave as she had insinuated. "Okay, I'll leave that alone for now, but I stopped by for another reason."

Standing her ground at the door, she retorted, "I don't have all day, Jimmy. Say what you came to say and get out of here."

"I can't help but notice you're still holding on to this old place. I mean, what's keeping you here? There's nothing for you in this town anymore."

"What business is it of yours?"

"Probably none, but considering we have a past, I wanted to offer to help you sell this place so you could move back to Pittsburgh."

Lydia moved aside so a customer could enter the shop and whispered, "I'm not interested in selling. And even if I were, you'd be the last person I'd hire to represent me."

"Ouch! That's a bit harsh, don't you think? I'm just trying

to help."

"I don't need your help," she muttered through clenched teeth. "And I certainly don't trust you to handle something so important."

Before Jimmy could answer, Aaron walked in, giving Lydia a questioning glance, asking, "Problem here?"

With a final smirk, Jimmy shouted, "Nothing but a little business, and the last thing I need is some two-bit Amish guy poking his nose into things that don't concern him."

Jimmy wasn't afraid of Aaron Shetler, even though he stood almost six inches taller and outweighed him by fifty pounds. However, when Aaron took a step closer, Jimmy couldn't help but step back, but not before adding, "Go ahead," he taunted, "take a swing. I know you want to but won't according to the silly rules you must abide." Jimmy tried to stand taller next to Aaron's towering frame and hissed. "I won her over last time, and I plan on winning again."

Lydia stepped between them. "Get out of here," she snapped in his face so close; he felt her breath on his chin.

Jimmy shrugged. "Suit yourself. But remember, Lydia, I'm your answer to getting out of this backward town if you change your mind."

As the door closed on his heels, Jimmy staggered away, mumbling under his breath, "You almost ruined my life once, Lydia Troyer; I'm not about to let you do it again."

***

Lydia couldn't close the door fast enough, and Aaron asked, "What was that all about?"

"He's pressuring me to sell. Says there's nothing for me here."

Aaron wrinkled his eyes together. "That doesn't sound like something he'd do out of the kindness of his heart. What is he really after?"

"My thoughts exactly," Lydia muttered. "I don't trust him after everything I've been through with him."

Aaron snapped, "Guys like that always have their own agenda."

Lydia returned to the counter, shaking her head and whispering, "I can't believe I ever allowed myself to fall for someone like him."

Aaron followed her to the counter and pined, "And I can't believe I let you…"

When he didn't say it loud enough for her to hear, she turned and asked, "Did you say something?"

"No... nothing that matters anyways."

She smiled and asked, "Did you come to work on the bathroom again this morning?"

"No, I stopped by to tell you I won't be able to work for a couple of days. Mattie Rose is under the weather, and I better stay close to the house. *Mamm* is with her right now, tending to her sore throat."

"Oh no! What can I do to help?"

"I was hoping you could pick out a couple of new books for her, and I was thinking a visit from Yankee might lift her spirits."

"Yankee would love to spend the day with her." Lydia handed him Yankee's lead and exclaimed, "How about I get a few things together for her this afternoon and come out and deliver them personally? I may even get her some ice cream from the Dairy Bar. Would she like that?"

"Like it? She'll be your friend forever."

"Good. I'll be out right after I close for the day."

Aaron snapped on the lead to Yankee's collar. "Do you think you can handle supper from a guy whose mac and cheese comes from a box and hotdogs are a staple on his table?"

Lydia giggled. "I'll do you one better. How about you let me cook for you both tonight? I'll make something that Mattie Rose won't have trouble swallowing."

Aaron had a hard time concealing the relief that rushed over him with the chance to get a homecooked meal. "I'm not going to turn you down," he snickered.

***

When Lydia left her car carrying a tote of groceries and Mattie's ice cream, a sense of familiarity washed over her as she approached Aaron's house. The warm summer evening air carried the scent of freshly spread manure, and the distant sound of cows mooing in the distance added to the peaceful country surroundings. Setting the bag down on the porch, she gently knocked on the door, then she waited, a flutter of excitement in her chest.

After a few seconds, Aaron opened the door, a warm smile spreading across his face. "A welcome visit for hungry souls." He picked up the bag and stood aside as she entered.

"I hope you're not too hungry because what I have planned

will take a little bit to get on the table," she inserted as she walked over to Mattie Rose, who was curled up on the couch with a book and an array of faceless dolls. "This is melting, so you best eat it up quickly." Laying her hand on her forehead, she gave Aaron a worrisome glance.

Mattie Rose looked up at her father for his approval. "Go ahead… but just this once," he said.

Lydia crouched down beside her. "How are you feeling today?"

Mattie Rose looked up, her eyes brightening at her. "Hurts," she muttered as she pointed to her throat.

Lydia reached over and tucked a loose hair behind her ear out of the way of a big spoon of ice cream heading for her mouth. "Well, I brought you a few things to help you feel better." She rummaged through her bag and pulled out a couple of books and a small stuffed bear, offering it to the little girl.

Without saying a word, Mattie Rose exchanged the cup of ice cream for the bear, pulling it close to her chest.

With Aaron's and Mattie Rose's smiles, Lydia couldn't shake the overwhelming contentment that washed over her. For some reason, despite her challenges, being there with Aaron and Mattie Rose felt like coming home. And as she glanced at them both, she couldn't help but feel grateful for the unexpected bond that was forming between them.

As Aaron moved toward the kitchen, Lydia followed him to the kitchen and muttered, "She's got a fever."

"*Jah*, I just gave her something for it," he sighed. "It's those tonsils again. Dr. Smithson says they need to come out."

Lydia moved around the kitchen, and before too long, the aroma of chicken and dumplings penetrated the air, mingling with the warmth of Aaron's cozy home. Aaron sat at the table, his brow furrowing into a troubled crease. "Frannie was always the one to make big decisions like this. I just don't know the right thing to do when it comes to doctoring the girl. My *mamm* says one thing, and the doctor says another."

Lydia checked on the chicken before sitting beside him at the table. "I'm sure it's a hard decision, especially on your own."

Aaron looked over at Lydia, looking for her opinion. "I know you've never had children and probably don't know the turmoil a parent must face with such things, but what do you think?"

A lump formed in the back of Lydia's throat so big it nearly shut off all the air to her lungs, and it took her a moment to gather her thoughts. He was right. She didn't know what to do, but she knew a parent's turmoil. She had lived it every day for the past four years. She turned back to Mattie Rose and his present concern, only after Aaron whispered her name. "I just... I don't know either, but if Mattie Rose were mine, I would do whatever it took to ease her pain once and for all."

Lydia stood up, and Aaron looked up at her, gratitude shining. "Thanks, I needed to hear that. I've been thinking that if the doctor says they need to come out, he'd know best."

Throughout the rest of the evening, her secret lingered on her shoulders, a burden she couldn't shake. As they sat down for supper, she found herself stealing glances at Aaron, her mind consumed by the thought of revealing her deepest secret. She wondered how he would react, whether he would be understanding or if it would drive a wedge between their two worlds.

***

Jimmy shut the door to his office and picked up the phone to dial Ben Markle's number.

"Ben, it's Jimmy Scott. We need to talk about the properties on Main Street."

"I take it you have some news for me?" Markle asked.

"No, not yet. I'm still working on it. But I need to tell you Lydia Troyer will be a bigger issue than I thought."

Ben groaned. "What's holding her to that old building?"

Jimmy shifted the phone to his other ear. "What you don't understand about these people is that they hold tight to tradition and family legacies."

Ben snorted a laugh. "For Pete's sake, they're not cavemen who don't know the value of money. Anyone, even the Amish, can be bought for the right price."

"I'm not ready to give up just yet," Jimmy inserted. "I've not had much luck getting back into Lydia's good graces, but her brother Harvey may be another story altogether."

"Giving up isn't an option," Ben snapped. "We're running out of time. If I don't get my hands on those buildings soon, my whole operation will be in jeopardy, and then you'll have bigger problems than dealing with your father."

Jimmy's character turned as serious as he could muster. "I told you I was working on it. Let me go out and talk to her brother. I'm certain I can make some headway with him."

Ben let the silence loiter among them for a few seconds

before adding, "And don't forget I hold more cards from your past than you may be willing to bet on just yet."

Jimmy held his breath, hoping Mr. Markle had forgotten the one little piece of his past that could ruin any chance he might have of taking over his father's business one day. "You wouldn't dare," Jimmy mumbled.

"Try me. You know I always get what I want. And right now, I want those buildings."

Jimmy's jaw twitched as he realized the extent of Ben's power over his future. "I'll do whatever it takes," he countered, clenching the phone to his ear.

"See to it that you do, and work on getting that girl back down here. I must admit she's gotten under my skin, and I want her back sitting at her desk."

***

Ben Markle's frustration peaked; he paced the length of his high-rise Pittsburgh office, his mind churning with possibilities. He'd long grown weary of waiting for Jimmy to fulfill his wishes. He reached for his phone to cancel his afternoon appointments, his mind already formulating a plan of action. He knew he held a powerful weapon in his possession—the knowledge of Lydia's past, of the child she gave up for adoption. It was a secret he'd held onto for the exact moment in time where it could benefit him the most. He didn't want to use it, but she left him no choice. Lydia didn't come to Markle Media by some wayward chance; it was all part of his long-term plan.

With a smug sense of resolution, he set to drive to Willow Springs and confront Lydia directly, lay his cards on the table, and leave it up to her to make the final decision. The building or his discretion about her sordid past.

***

Jimmy contemplated his next move as a cold determination consumed him. He wasn't willing to let Markle continue to sway over him; he couldn't allow him to use his past as a weapon against him. He needed to find a way to deal with him before things got out of hand. Jimmy steered himself ahead for the difficult task. He would do anything to protect his position at Scott Properties, even if it meant revealing what he knew about Lydia to her brother.

As he approached Harvey's barn office, he braced himself for the man's quick temper and unresolved manner. But he was willing to do what he needed to do, even if it meant tarnishing Lydia's reputation. Jimmy entered the man's office without being invited, his gaze locked on Harvey Troyer. "We need to talk."

Harvey took a second glance, then the recollection of where he might know him from settled on his face. "I can't imagine what kind of business I might have with you." Harvey sneered. "I'm pretty sure I said all I needed to say to you five years ago when I chased you away from my sister."

Jimmy pulled his shoulders back. "And how did that work out for you? If I remember, she picked me over your empty threats."

"What's this about?" Harvey demanded, his words flat and to the point.

"I want to discuss the building on Main Street that your father owns. I have a client who's interested in purchasing it. I've already spoken to your sister, but she isn't interested in hearing me out."

Harvey tipped back in his chair. "Go on, I'm listening."

Jimmy wrote a figure on the blank notepad that lay on the

desk. "My client is ready to offer you that amount."

"Have you shown her that offer?" Harvey inquired.

"No, I can barely get past the front door. That's why I'm here. I'm figuring you might have more pull with her, at least considering such a generous offer."

"What makes you so sure I have any influence? I'm pretty sure my father left the building to her. I just haven't been able to find proof of that, and until I do, there isn't much I can do."

Jimmy took a seat and scoffed. "You see, that's where I might be able to help you twist her arm some."

Harvey's eyes narrowed, his jaw tightening in response to Jimmy's comment. "How so?" he asked.

Jimmy hesitated, knowing that revealing Lydia's secret would end any chance of her ever giving him a second chance. But he also knew it was the only way to escape Markle's threats.

"I hold some information you and your family might like to know about your sweet little sister. I know firsthand she isn't as innocent as you thought she was... even if I had to force the issue somewhat." Harvey was clearly bothered by what he was insinuating, but Jimmy persisted before he lost his nerve. "I'd highly suggest you convince her to consider my client's offer, or I may let it slip all I know about her visit to the Woman's

Center for Unwed Mothers."

"Out!" Harvey bellowed, his voice bouncing off the cement walls. "Get out of here before I make you regret stepping foot on my property."

The air in the room grew tense, but Jimmy couldn't deny his satisfaction in finally getting one over on the Troyer family. He pushed the figure closer to Harvey as his smirk widened. "What will it be, old man? Money or pride?" Harvey pointed to the door, and Jimmy walked away, feeling complete in setting the wheels in motion again.

Harvey sat alone in the dimly lit room, his heart pounding in his ears with a sickening sense of dread settling in the pit of his being. His mind raced with a thousand questions about what Jimmy implied, and he struggled to understand what he had just heard.

How on earth would he ever be able to confront his sister with such a delicate matter? The mere thought of what she had to endure alone sent a shiver down his spine. He might not be happy that she returned to Willow Springs, but she was still his *schwester*, and what Jimmy alluded to was almost too much to bear.

The thought of Jimmy admitting so callously to the part he played in her running away made his skin crawl. More than that, he knew that he would never go to the police with such information; it just wasn't their way.

Harvey knew he couldn't rest until he had the answers, but the prospect of confronting Lydia with what he knew left him sick with her past, and his own simmering guilt.

With a heavy sigh, he knew he couldn't continue to keep his own secrets if he demanded an explanation from Lydia. He had to find a way to deal with both Jimmy Scott's threats and the current state of his affairs. He walked to the door and checked where his *bruders* were before retrieving his cell phone from its hiding spot. It was time he took things in his own hands.

CHAPTER 10

The Sandwich Shoppe was the perfect place to meet over lunch to formulate a plan to save Main Street. As Lydia sat across from Ruthie, she couldn't help but smile and hush her spirited personality.

"Shhhh..." Lydia whispered, "I understand your frustration, Ruthie. I'm just as bothered by the way Scott Properties is trying to convince everyone to sell, but you need to be quiet. We don't need the whole town up in arms about this."

Ruthie leaned forward, her eyes sparkling with determination. "We can't just sit back and let them bulldoze their own agenda throughout the community. If the merchants start selling off one by one, what will happen to Willow Springs?"

Lydia nodded in agreement. "I know, but we need to approach this delicately. We can't afford to alarm the business owners until we have all our ducks in a row; we'll cause unnecessary panic."

In typical Ruthie fashion, she waved a dismissive hand. "Don't worry about that, I've already got a plan in motion," she announced. "We'll organize a secret meeting of the Amish Main Street Business Association and lay out the facts about the hidden passageways that run under the street connecting each business to the next. Once they see the potential for increased tourism and business, they'll all come together and agree not to sell out. If we let just one business go, we're doomed."

Lydia couldn't help but admire Ruthie's boldness, even if she felt a pang of apprehension. "I hope you're right, but we must keep things quiet until we're ready to reveal it all at once.

"Let Aaron and me gather more information first. I haven't had a chance to review my father's records on the subject. There's more at risk than just locating the tunnels. We found proof that some underhanded activity may be going on below the surface of Willow Springs that must be stopped first."

As Lydia and Ruthie discussed their plans, Lydia felt someone watching them. When she lifted her head to take a sip of her coffee, she noticed Ed Glick lurking behind the coffee counter, his eyes fixed on her with an unsettling force. When Lydia caught his eyes, he smirked, tipped his head in her direction, and went back to fill the coffee carafe.

"Ruthie, what do you know about Ed Glick?" Lydia whispered.

Ruthie followed Lydia's eyes to the counter. "Oh, him. I've heard a few things, none of them good. Word has it, he's not the most trustworthy person. Always pushing the boundaries of the *Ordnung,* ya know? I heard he's had more than one run-in with the bishop."

Lydia frowned. "Something about him makes my skin crawl. He's up to something; I just can't put my finger on what."

Ruthie shrugged. "It's hard to say, but if your gut tells you to stay clear… I'd do just that."

Lydia gently stirred more sugar into her coffee, her mind trying to push Ed's obvious attention in her to the back of her mind. "I've been thinking about creating a section in the bookshop dedicated to the history of Willow Springs. It would be nice to show Main Street's part in the underground railroad. I've already ordered more books and chronicles on the subject."

Ruthie's eyes lit up with excitement. "That's a great idea! And I could do something similar. I have a collection of old cookbooks from around the Civil War that I could display. I've been collecting them for years, but they're stored in an old chest upstairs."

Lydia reached over and laid her hand over Ruthie's. "But we need to keep it quiet until we have a chance to meet with the other merchants."

"Of course," Ruthie inserted.

***

Ed rudely dismissed his coworker and headed to the back stairs leading to the Sandwich Shoppe's basement. Grabbing his backpack off the hook by the back door as he passed, his mind was consumed with the task at hand. He needed to retrieve the books from the cellar and replace them with replicas while Lydia was in the coffee shop.

Ignoring the protests of his coworkers about the shop being too busy for him to take a break, he hurried down the steps and into the darkest corner of the cold and damp basement.

Retrieving a flashlight from his bag, he entered the dark tunnel, his steps quick and purposeful. He pushed the heavy bookshelf open to reveal the bookshop cellar and flashed his light toward the glass case he had smashed the week before. His frustration simmered just below the surface as he couldn't see where the books had been moved. He cursed under his breath, knowing Harvey would not be pleased with his failure to retrieve the valuable books as instructed. Their buyer would be furious if he didn't present more original copies. He cussed at his choice to smash the case since he had lost the key.

Finding where the books might have been moved, he looked around the cellar, knocking over a stack of plastic totes and making a thunderous racket. He recognized the familiar bark of Lydia's dog, and his frustration intensified.

"Stupid mutt," he muttered under his breath. He hoped to slip in and out of the Book Cellar unnoticed, but it seemed fate had other plans. With a disgusted sigh, he returned to the passageway the same way he entered, knowing that his mission would have to wait for another day.

Meanwhile, Lydia and Ruthie resumed discussing their planned meeting at the coffee shop, unaware of Ed taking the opportunity to enter the bookshop. As they chatted, Lydia's ears perked up at Yankee's booming warning.

"Excuse me, Ruthie, I think that's Yankee barking. I'd better get back and see what he's so worked up about."

Ruthie nodded understandingly. "Certainly. I need to get the bakery opened as well. A few *Englisch* women are coming for a baking class this morning."

With a quick goodbye, Lydia returned next door, trying to push the sense of dread aside every step along the way.

Stepping into the bookshop, she found Yankee standing at the closed cellar door, his hackles raised and a low growl rumbling in his throat. She approached cautiously, her heart jumping out of her chest as she picked up a flashlight and pushed open the door to descend the steps.

She flashed the light over the front area, and nothing seemed amiss, but as she treaded quietly into the back corner, she saw the toppled totes and sighed with relief. As she worked to stack the overturned containers back up, her eyes landed on something glinting on the floor near Yankee's paw. With unease, she bent down to examine it, her fingers trembling as she picked it up.

It was a toothpick, slightly chewed and bearing the faint scent of tobacco. All at once, she realized the significance of the discarded piece of evidence. The toothpick hinted at someone's recent visit to the cellar, raising new questions about who had been there and why.

Yankee's sudden growl forced Lydia to follow him to the back wall, where he stood rumbling before an old built-in bookshelf. Lydia's heart raced as she stared at the inconspicuous wall unit; her mind consumed with what might be lurking behind it.

A chill swept through the air, and she quickly called to Yankee to follow her as every instinct told her to flee the cellar as fast as her legs could carry her.

Back upstairs, she reached for her cell phone just as the front door opened to reveal Ben Markle's boisterous form sucking the life out of the shop. Even though his smile was charming and inviting, Lydia sensed his visit was anything but.

"Mr. Markle, what are you doing here? I thought we had settled the issue of me coming back to work."

"We have, but I was in the area, so I thought I'd give it one last try. You can't stop a man from trying to go after what he wants." He sloped in a little too close, his manner turning more intimate. "And you know it's you I want most."

"Ben, please," she said firmly, stepping back to put distance between them. "And I've told you on more than one occasion I'm not interested in what you have to offer."

No doubt, the change in Lydia's attitude offended him, and the air in the room shifted as his demeanor took on a more sinister feeling. As if a switch had been flipped, his voice turned cold, and his face hardened as he pulled a brochure from his pocket and laid it on the counter. The image of a pregnant woman and the brochure cover dug a hole in Lydia's heart, and she gasped at the business name clearly printed across the top of the folded card stock. "Seems I hit you exactly where I need you," he sneered.

It took Lydia a few seconds to settle the bile rising in her throat before she could respond. "What do you want?"

Ben sat on the stool on the opposite side of the counter and put the brochure back in his pocket before replying. "Let's just say you have something I want, and I won't think twice about using what I know to get what I want."

He waited until she composed her mounting anger before adding, "I'd say the ball is in your court. You can sell me this building, come back to work for me, and this little tidbit of information will disappear. Or you can lose your precious reputation, which I hear will land you in a heap of trouble with your family and this precious Amish community you've tried to fit back into." He unwrapped a stick of gum and chewed it smoothly as he patiently waited for her answer.

In all that she'd been through, she couldn't think of another time in her life when she despised someone as much as she did right at that moment. The gravity of his threats crushed her spirit. She always feared the day would come when her past would come back to haunt her, but she never imagined she'd have to explain herself to the likes of Ben Markle.

Before she could respond, the heavy door creaked open, and Aaron and Detective Powers entered the shop. Lydia's breath caught in respite at the unexpected visit.

Aaron must have sensed her discomfort and demanded. "What's going on here?"

Detective Powers stepped forward, his gaze following Ben. "Well, isn't this interesting? You're just the person of interest we've been investigating. Seems Jimmy Scott let the cat out of the bag in one too many places about your connection to the attention forming in the old building along Main Street."

"What of it?" Markle scoffed. "I have a bonified curiosity in real estate. The last time I checked, that isn't a crime."

"Perhaps not," the detective added. "But we have reason to believe your motives are not entirely above the board."

Ben gave them all a dismissive grunt as he stood to leave. "If you have something more substantial than your instincts, you can contact my lawyer, but other than that, I don't need to entertain any of this a minute longer."

Detective Powers stood in front of him and glared sternly at him. "I have enough evidence to call you in for questioning about some underhanded activity happening throughout Willow Springs. We can do it here or back at the station. Your choice."

"You've got to be kidding." Markle spat.

"Good. Then, you have nothing to worry about if we take this conversation to the station."

As they both walked toward the door, Ben turned back toward Lydia. "I take it you'll consider my offer."

Lydia exchanged anxious glances with Markle, her suspicions about his true motives evident on his face, only reinforced by the detective's pointed questions. As they departed the store, she took a silent, cleansing breath and turned to face Aaron. She may have secrets about her past, but she refused to allow them to control her future.

***

The room had an unsettling heaviness as Aaron scrutinized Lydia's reaction to Markle's comment. However, how she quickly changed the subject the minute they left gave him the impression it wasn't the time to dwell on it. Instead, he redirected her focus on the last of the repairs to the bathroom. "I was hoping to finish things up today while my *mamm* is watching Mattie Rose."

Lydia nodded, grateful for the distraction, and recounted the unsettling encounter with Yankee and the cellar earlier. As she spoke, Aaron listened and knew they had to get to the bottom of the strange occurrences.

"Can you close the shop for a bit while we check things out?"

"Sure, it's been a slow day. Let me turn the sign and lock the door first."

Aaron studied her carefully and couldn't help but notice the slight tremble in her hands as she flipped the sign. "Maybe we'll find some answers down there," he stated.

As they both stood before the built-in bookcase, Yankee began to grumble a long stare at the almost bare old bookshelf. "Looks like Yankee sees or hears something beyond our comprehension." Aaron started to run his hand along the edge of the case, looking for a hidden lever or button. When nothing turned up, Lydia started to study the few books positioned oddly on the top shelf. When she tried to tip the largest book toward her case, she heard a click, and the bookcase released itself from the wall. "Wow!" Aaron exclaimed. "You found it."

They stood back and let the cool, musty air cover them like a blanket immersed in the dark tunnel. Aaron shined a flash of light into the old passageway. "Looks like we found our answer," Aaron remarked, a sense of conclusion washing over him as he started to piece together a slew of unanswered questions. "The broken window, the locked doors—it all makes sense now."

"What now?" Lydia asked.

Aaron pushed the entry point closed. "We get the detective back down here to look things over. I'd hate for us to disturb any evidence we might come across."

Lydia pulled the toothpick from her jeans pocket. "I found this today."

"And you think it's important?" he asked.

"I'm not sure, but I think I know who it might belong to."

Aaron scratched his short beard as she gave him her thoughts. "Now that puts a whole new spin on things, doesn't it? But it also puts more suspicion on your *bruder*."

"Exactly. That's why I didn't mention it to Detective Powers before he left. It wasn't the right time to discuss that with him."

Taking great care with the shards of glass littering the floor, they both worked on cleaning up the broken bookcase that stored her father's collection of books. As Lydia carefully removed the shattered glass, her fingers brushed against something unexpected—a small hidden compartment under the bottom shelf.

"Hey, Aaron, look at this," she exclaimed, her voice barely audible as she pointed to the locked compartment.

"That's an odd place for a secret hiding place," his brow furrowed as he examined her discovery. "What do you think is in it?"

She tugged at the handle. "At this point, I wouldn't be surprised by anything my father has kept hidden." She turned the handle, but its resistance kept her from discovering what might be inside. "There must be something important in there since it's locked up tight. Remember that key I showed you that came with *Datt's* journal? Maybe the key belongs to this drawer."

Aaron nodded in agreement, his mind already racing with the possibilities to unravel more of the secrets of her father's passing. "Let's finish cleaning this mess up first," he suggested. "Then we can see if that key matches the lock."

Lydia ran her fingers along the hidden compartment, hesitating long enough to sense that the contents were meant for her eyes only. She knew she would need to wait until Aaron left before retrieving the key she had stored away with her father's journal. It felt like a secret her father had entrusted to her alone, and she wasn't ready to share it with Aaron yet.

With a cleansing breath, she emptied the last dustpan full of shattered glass into the waiting bin and exclaimed, "Since I've closed the shop early for the day, I think I'd like to go out and check on Mattie Rose. I got in a few new books for her."

Aaron chuckled. "You're spoiling the girl, but she'll love it." He headed up the stairs, carrying the heavy tub of glass. "But no more ice cream before supper," he laughed.

Happy she was able to take his attention away from the locked drawer, she grabbed Yankee's lead and led them both out of the shop. "Let me stop at the store, and I'll be right behind you," she inserted.

In a lighthearted statement, he asked, "You wouldn't happen to be planning on one of your wonderful meals again, would you?"

She gave him a lingering smile. "You read my mind. I hope you don't mind. I love to cook, and you need to eat. I'd say it's a perfect combination, don't you?"

He laughed and waved her off as he walked to his secured buggy across the street. "See you soon," he hollered.

Knowing he would want to get back to Mattie Rose, she was glad her plan had diverted his attention long enough that he didn't offer her a ride. A stop at the store was just the thing she needed to make sure she'd be returning to the shop alone later.

Tracy Fredrychowski

CHAPTER 11

Lydia stood before the bookcase; her eyes drawn to the hidden compartment concealed below the bottom shelf. How her father ever thought she'd find his hiding spot without the case being smashed was beyond her. However, she couldn't help but think that some of the mysterious entries she found in his journal would have led her to the discovery at some point.

With a mix of curious apprehension, she reached for the key her father had sent her, and considered the weight in her hand. She sucked in a breath and prayed it would fit the lock. There was a moment of hesitation, as if the lock wanted to resist the intrusion, before finally giving way with a soft click.

She opened the lid and prayed that whatever secrets lay hidden beneath the surface would give them more clues into her father's untimely death. As she positioned the flashlight on the floor so she could use both hands to sift through the contents, she exhaled an agonizing moan when the only thing in the drawer was a newspaper article. Lydia's breath caught in her throat as she read the question her father had scribbled on the side of the yellowed paper. LYDIA'S?

Lydia gingerly lifted the newspaper in front of the light, and her heart seemed to stop beating for a few moments as she studied it. The image revealed a tiny bundle wrapped in the unique baby quilt her mother had made before her birth. The treasured heirloom, a piece of her mother she carried around until the time she went to school, was her most cherished possession. That was until she passed it on to her own daughter on the day she handed her over to the adoption agency.

Undoubtedly, if her father had seen the article, he would have recognized the quilt with its distinctive design in the shape of a sunflower, her mother's favorite flower. The article didn't mention the names of the adoptive parents; it only highlighted the adoption agency and the work they do to match childless couples with children in the greater Pittsburgh area.

For years, Lydia carried the weight of her decision alone, burying the pain of her daughter's absence hidden in her heart. And now, before her, was a hard reminder of the child she had been forced to give up—the child she had never stopped loving despite the years of separation.

Lydia traced her fingertip over her daughter's outline on the fading newspaper as a flood of memories washed over her. The joy of holding her squirming newborn, even when they advised against it, and the sorrow of saying goodbye when she handed her off. The ache of her longing never truly faded.

With tears streaming down her face, Lydia murmured a silent promise to her daughter that she would always love her and pray that her life would be sealed with joy no matter where she was. Lydia laid a tender kiss on top of the photo and pulled it to her chest, allowing years of built-up regret to gush away with her tears.

Yankee laid his head gently in her lap as she sat on her knees in front of the open box. Feeling the warmth of his body on her legs, Lydia let out a shuddering breath, her hand reaching out to stroke his head in a silent gesture of gratitude.

With Yankee at her side, she carried the box upstairs, locked the photo back in it, and tucked it safely away before crawling into bed for the night.

***

Harvey sat beside Edna at the breakfast table and explained

what he'd discovered about Lydia.

"I'm just saying, I can't ignore the facts," Harvey insisted, his voice full of frustration. "How can you think she'd ever make her way back amongst the People if word of her indiscretion got back to the bishop and ministers?"

Edna stirred more sugar in her coffee than her ample frame needed, saying, "I think you're being too hard on the girl. Hasn't she been through enough?"

"Don't you see woman!" he snapped. "If she leaves, we can sell that property and be done with it. So many things could get resolved if we just rid ourselves of that place, not to mention, we've been offered a pretty price for it."

Edna backed away and snapped back. "You're like a bomb about ready to explode."

"You seem to forget," he sneered, "it's your hide as well as everyone else's who counts on this farm to support their families."

Edna raised her hands. "I'm so done with this. First, it was the journal, then the books, and now the building… you've got yourself so tied up in knots about all this you're not good to anyone, especially me!"

Harvey waved a dismissive hand, weariness in his tone.

"What do you know about anything? You didn't have to deal with my father over any of this. It wasn't you who tried to talk sense into the old man who couldn't grasp anything but his hope for his precious daughter to come home." Harvey ran his hand through his thinning hair in exasperation. "If only I could get my hands on that journal."

Enda moved to the stove to check on the bacon. "And what if he left the store to Lydia? Wouldn't that make sense? All you boys already have farms of your own, and none of you took any notice of the bookshop."

Havery stood and grabbed his straw hat from the back door peg. "I've lost my appetite, and I have work to do; I can't waste any more time on this right now." He opened the bag Edna had placed near the back door and asked, "Did you pick up more rat poison at the hardware?"

"*Jah*, I left it in the box on the porch; I didn't want that nasty stuff in my kitchen." The screen door slammed behind him as he took long, strong strides toward the barn, mumbling along the way. "One way or another, *schwester*, you're going to be out of my hair; you just made my job easier with what I know now." Just as he treaded into the barn, Joshua pulled up beside the double doors, hopped down from his buggy cart, and secured it to the hitching post, calling out to him. "Harvey."

He heaved a sigh and kept on walking into the barn, confident he would follow if he wanted to talk. Dealing with his youngest *bruder* was the last thing he had patience for.

"Harvey?" Joshua hollered. "We need to talk about Lydia."

"That's the last person I want to talk about. The girl is a thorn in my side, and I wish she would have stayed away."

"What is it about her that is bothering you so much?" Joshua probed. "Thank goodness she returned, or we would have had to close the store."

"Exactly!"

Joshua followed him into his office and shut the door. "Look, we all know *Datt* hoped she would return and take over the store. That wasn't a surprise to any of us. Why are you having trouble with that? It's what *Datt* wanted."

Harvey slapped his hand down on his desk. "She'll never be accepted back into the community, and she needs to leave before it's too late, and I'm going to tell her as much."

"What are you talking about?" Joshua asked.

Harvey sat and leaned back in his chair, sucking in a long breath. "Let's just say I discovered a circumstance that forced her to leave home."

Joshua's brow creased. "What do you mean?"

In a grave utterance, Harvey replied, "She was with child when she left. And not only that, but she also gave that child up for adoption."

Harvey's' revelation hung in the air, forcing Joshua to sink into the chair at the desk. His eyes were wide with disbelief. "But... why didn't she tell us?"

Harvey shook his head, a bitter tone taking hold. "Could it be that *Englisch* boy, Jimmy Scott, and her were too ashamed to admit to it? But the fact remains that she's been living with this secret for years, and now it's catching up with her."

Joshua took off his hat and ran his hand through his hair. "So, what do you plan to do?"

Harvey's jaw clenched. "I plan to make her see reason and let us sell the store. She can't stay, not with this hanging over her head; the People will never accept her back into the fold."

"She'll be heartbroken; she had resolved to stay."

"If she doesn't leave willingly, then I'm prepared to use this knowledge to force her hand in the matter," Harvey said harshly.

***

Lydia stood at the counter sorting through a new order as Harvey marched in, his countenance and steps determined. He stood inside the doorway, and Lydia observed as his eyes darted around the entire shop. "We need to talk," he demanded as he approached the counter.

She glanced around the store and uttered, "I'm pretty busy... can it wait thirty minutes until I close up shop?"

Harvey stood in denial at her request and didn't budge until she nodded toward the stairs that led to her apartment. "Go upstairs, and I'll be there as soon as I close the store." He looked past the line of customers at the counter and grumbled under his breath as he headed to the stairs. "I made some iced tea earlier, and it's in the refrigerator. Help yourself," she added, hoping to soften the lines across his forehead.

***

It worked for Harvey as he peered around Lydia's apartment while waiting for her to close the store. The eeriness of his father's existence attached itself in every corner of the small place. While rummaging through a stack of books near his chair, he caught sight of the stack of old books arranged neatly on the kitchen table. His pulse quickened as he stopped looking for the journal and concentrated on the collection. Without hesitation, he removed his hat and tucked two of the smaller books under it, hoping to retrieve them as soon as he left.

Yankee stretched, moved from his napping spot under the window, and stood at Harvey's side, wagging his tail in the hope of some attention. Harvey brushed him away just as Lydia ran upstairs.

"I closed as soon as the last customer left. What is so important that you had to make a spectacle like that? Is everything okay?"

"No, Lydia, everything is not okay. In fact, it's far from it." He moved around the front of the table and lowered his voice in an ominous rumble. "I know about your secret, little *schwester*. About why you had to leave Willow Springs."

Lydia sank into her father's chair. "How... how could you know about that?"

"It doesn't really matter how I know. What matters now is how we handle the situation and what it means for your future in Willow Springs."

Harvey watched as all the color drained from Lydia's face as she brought her hands up to her chin and exhaled. "Harvey, please, I… I had my reasons for what I did. I was given no other option, and I thought it was best for everyone involved."

"Well, your reason really doesn't change what you did and why you can't stay here. You need to leave Willow Springs before word of this gets any further than this family."

Lydia swallowed hard and asked, "Who… who else knows?"

"Just Edna and Joshua so far, but certain people won't think twice about letting the cat out of the bag unless they get what they want."

"And what's that?" she asked nervously.

"This building, for one," Harvey stated.

Lydia's eyes plugged with tears. "But what about the bookshop? *Datt* left it to me, Harvey. It's all I have left of him."

Harvey's fears were just realized by Lydia's statement, and he asked, "What makes you so sure those were his wishes?"

Lydia jumped up from the chair and retrieved their father's journal from the top of the cupboard. "He told me as much in his journal." She turned to the page that outlined who she needed to contact at the bank and which lawyer held the transfer deed. "See right here. *Datt* outlined his wishes, and I've already contacted the lawyer. The paperwork is final."

Harvey tried to grab the book from her hands, but she twisted away as she spat. "Absolutely not! He sent this to me. He would have shared it with you if he wanted you to see what was in it."

Lydia put the table between them and inserted, "I'm not leaving, Harvey. The store and this building are mine, and if it takes the whole world knowing my business, then so be it. You... Ben Markle, and even Jimmy Scott, have no hold over me, and I won't be bullied by any of you into selling what is rightfully mine."

Harvey could feel the blood rising to his cheeks at her bold denial. "You'll never be accepted here, Lydia. You'll be an outcast, and even Aaron Shelter won't want anything to do with you once he finds out you're used."

Harvey watched her process his words as his anger simmered beneath the surface. He took a step closer. "You're making a mistake. If you don't see things my way, then you'll leave me no choice but to go to the bishop and reveal the truth to the church leaders."

"What makes you think that makes a difference in my world? I couldn't care less what the bishop thinks. He has no hold over me or my decisions. Do you fail to remember I never joined the church?" She hesitated before lashing out again. "Furthermore, what makes you think I would ever join the Amish church again? I've tasted the real world, and I have no desire to fall prey to the *Ordnung* ever again."

"Perhaps not, but you need to remember Aaron is a church member and falls under our rules and traditions. You'll be exposing him to all sorts of turmoil." Harvey moved so close he was sure she felt his breath on her face. "You might not care about tarnishing your own reputation... but what about his?"

"I can't speak for Aaron, but I hope he will stand by me when he hears the truth about what really happened."

Harry snorted a laugh. "Oh, I heard it all from Jimmy. How he had to force himself on you, but I look at it as you shouldn't have allowed yourself to get into a situation where that might happen. I hold you just as responsible."

Lydia squared her shoulders, stood firm, and spat back. "I won't back down without a fight."

Harvey lowered his voice to a grumble, so much so that Yankee moved to Lydia's side as he said, "You're being naïve. Can you go up against Ben Markle and Jimmy Scott's family and come out ahead? You have no idea what they are capable of."

He grabbed his hat, careful to keep the two books he'd tucked inside concealed as he turned to leave. "I'll give you a few days to calm down. But you best think long and hard about what this might do to your family's reputation in the community and Aaron Shetler's life if you decide to stay."

Lydia held her breath until she heard the heavy front door open and close. Only then did she allow herself to collapse back in her father's chair and cry. The ominous occurrence of her *bruder* stayed in the air long after he left, and she couldn't shake the impression that her darkest days were yet to come.

***

The next evening, with Harvey's visit still hanging heavy in the air, Lydia exhaled as Aaron entered the bookshop with Detective Powers.

With a welcoming smile pasted on his lips, Aaron announced, "We waited until we were sure the store was closing before we came by. I told Lewis we had found the hidden doorway, and he wants to look closer."

Lydia wasn't in the mood for anything of such. She only

wanted to retreat to her apartment and shut out the world. But as Aaron and the detective exchanged excited glances, she knew she couldn't dampen their enthusiasm. Summoning a halfhearted smile, she nodded in agreement.

The musty odor of old books penetrated the air as Lydia, Aaron, and Lewis huddled together in the dimly lit cellar. Dust danced in the glow of their large flashlight as Lydia led the way.

"The passage is right behind this bookshelf," she mentioned as she pulled the secret book down to unlatch its hold on the wall. Once the shelf was completely open, Aaron and the detective shone their lights down the long corridor.

The trio ventured into the darkness, and Aaron held the map Lydia had found in her father's belongings up to the light. He positioned the map in his hands to line up with the direction of the street above. Within a few seconds of entering the passageway, they reached a fork in the tunnel and stopped, waiting for Aaron's guidance. "Let's try the right path first. It seems wider, and according to the map, it leads under the parking lot over to the stables behind the storefronts."

With cautious steps, they studied the stone walls and looked for clues to who might know of the hidden areas below Willow Springs. When they came to a dead end, the detective cautiously pushed open a trapdoor in the ceiling. A few strands of straw fell to the dirt floor, and a ray of light filtered into the dark space. He peered through the tiny crack and whispered, "This leads to a stall in the stables." He paused and studied what he saw, then shut the door. "Too much activity in the stable to go unnoticed. Let's circle back and check out the other tunnel."

Detective Powers studied the walls and floor as they resumed their investigation. He ran his hand along the walls, looking for anything that might be concealed from the untrained eye. When his fingertips ran across an indention in the wall, he stopped and probed the outline until his fingers found the entrance. A small room, concealed behind a false wall, contained a stash of boxes and crates.

Lydia gasped at their findings as the detective carefully opened one of the boxes to discover a trove of contraband. Illegal firearms and packets of drugs neatly packed away. Aaron and Lydia exchanged grim looks. "This changes everything," Lewis exclaimed.

"What do you think it all means?" Lydia inquired.

"To begin with, it means that whoever is behind wanting to sell and purchase these buildings knows about these tunnels."

"And that list is growing longer and longer with each

passing day," Aaron added.

Lewis gently put the lid back on one of the crates. "I need to return to my office and report this immediately." As they returned through the tunnels and into the cellar, the detective asked, "Do either of you know how many of the other Main Street merchants have been contacted to sell?"

"All of them!" Lydia answered.

CHAPTER 12

A week later, Aaron resolved to try one more time to invite Lydia to spend time with him. His last attempt fell on deaf ears as she found an array of excuses to not be alone with him.

As he pulled up to the bookshop, his eyes immediately fell upon the cable installation van parked out front. Confusion draped over him as he inspected the technicians busy running cables and setting up equipment. After securing his buggy horse to the hitching post, he stepped on the sidewalk, gathering his thoughts before questioning Lydia about her plans.

With a determined stance, Aaron strode through the open door and made his way to the back of the shop, where the sound of a drill worked to bring the world into the mainly Amish bookshop. He looked around, unable to conceal the concern on his face. "Lydia?"

"Hello, Aaron," she replied with hesitation in her voice.

"What's going on here?"

Lydia moaned before she answered. "Exactly what it looks like. I'm bringing the shop into the twenty-first century."

"I can't help but feel uneasy about this," Aaron admitted, his voice barely above a whisper. He placed his hand under her elbow and guided her away from the service technician. "Adding Internet goes against our rules and traditions about connecting to the outside world."

"I know this is difficult for you, but you have to remember I'm not Amish," she reminded him gently but matter-of-factly. "I left those rules behind when I left the community." She stopped and looked up at him. "I must do what's best for the bookshop and my customers."

Aaron couldn't hide his discomfort. "But most of your customers are Amish, who shouldn't be subjecting themselves to such things."

"That's just it," she breathed. "I need to attract more *Englisch* patrons, and I can't do that without access to Wi-Fi. I also want to increase my online presence, offer eBooks, and even start shipping orders to customers who can't visit in person. To do that, I need reliable access."

A knot formed in the pit of Aaron's stomach. "I had...

hoped you might eventually return to your Amish roots. Seeing the Internet being installed here feels like that's another step away from that ever happening."

"Aaron, I can't make any promises about returning to the Amish way of life," she confessed softly. "But I promise I will always respect your beliefs and values, just as I hope you'll respect mine."

Aaron crossed his arms across his chest and rested back on the counter. "I'm worried about what it might do to the young people visiting the store. Bringing the Internet into the store could change the dynamic of our community. It might lead to distractions, temptations, and conflict with the bishop and the church leaders."

Lydia nodded slowly, her face dropping at his concern. "I hear your concerns, but embracing modern technology is essential for the bookshop's success. I'm committed to staying, and this is my only income… you have to understand I can't rely on anyone but myself and need to do this. Please, Aaron, I hoped you would understand that."

Their conversation was interrupted by a technician calling her over to answer placement instructions. Lydia gave him a reassuring smile and excused herself.

Aaron felt a sense of the tides changing as he watched Lydia at home in a world he knew little about. With a flicker of uncertainty, he met her eyes one last time before leaving. Deep down, he knew if he supported Lydia's changes, he would jeopardize his church membership.

***

Out of the corner of her eye, Lydia saw Aaron walk out of the shop and back into his buggy. His shoulders sank under the weight of her choices, and she couldn't help but feel a twinge of guilt gnawing at her conscience. She had no doubt she disappointed him, perhaps even dashed any hope he held for a future together with her. But entrenched in her soul, she knew their paths were moving apart, and there was little she could do to change that—it was only a matter of time before his judgment would come. For now, pushing him away seemed like the best option to spare them both from inevitable heartache.

As for Mattie Rose, her heart ached for the little girl who had become a source of joy in her life. She silently vowed to shield the girl from forming too strong an attachment to her, knowing that their time together might be fading.

***

A wave of exhaustion washed over Lydia as she closed the shop for the day. With Yankee by her side, she ventured out for a late afternoon walk, hoping the fresh air would clear her mind, consumed by Aaron's disapproving eyes. The park across the street seemed the perfect place to leave her heartache behind, if only for a few moments.

As she strolled along the winding paths and around the playground, the sound of children playing warmed her heart. Nearby, a small girl played in the sandbox, and when she caught sight of Yankee, she ran over, her eyes sparking with wonder. "Can I pet your dog?" she asked.

Lydia couldn't help but nod and smile at the girl's request. "Of course, his name is Yankee, and he loves children, especially little girls." A pang of regret remained as Lydia's mind turned toward Mattie Rose's love for the dog.

The little girl's mother hollered to get her attention, but the girl lingered by Lydia's side, not so happy about giving up their short visit. "You best go to your mommy," Lydia encouraged.

A short time later, Lydia came across the same young girl

187

sitting with her mother on a nearby bench. When Lydia walked past, the little girl begged, "Sit with us?"

Lydia looked to the girl's mother for her approval. "Please do," the woman said. "She can't stop talking about your dog, and we would love the company."

Lydia took a seat and welcomed the cheese cracker held out to her. "I love to share," the little girl added.

"Well, that's good because I love cheese crackers." Lydia leaned closer and said, "And you know who else loves crackers?"

The little girl's eyes brightened as Yankee gingerly took the offered cracker from her fingertips.

As they sat on the bench, Lydia couldn't help but perceive the young woman was distressed. Her coloring was pale, and she struggled to take in steady breaths. Before Lydia could inquire further, the little girl asked, "Mommy, can my new friend push me on the swing?"

"Oh… my dear. We can't impose like that. I'll push you shortly. Just let mommy catch her breath for a few minutes."

Lydia was quick to intervene. "If you don't mind, I would love to. Perhaps Yankee could sit with you?" Gratitude covered the woman's face as she took Yankee's lead while nodding her acceptance.

Instantly, the little girl slid her hand into Lydia's and led her to the swings. "What's your name?" she asked, her eyes shining with trust.

"Lydia, and yours?"

"Julia."

"Well, it's nice to meet you, Julia." As they walked across the playground, the little girl continued. "My mommy says I have to be brave because she's sick, and my daddy's gone away to live with Jesus."

For a moment, all the trouble Lydia was facing seemed nothing compared to the little girl's statement. She squeezed Julia's hand in reassurance. "You're a very brave girl, and I bet your mommy is lucky to have you taking care of her when she's not feeling well."

"She's been sick a long time, even before Daddy left."

"Oh, I'm sorry to hear that," Lydia inserted warmly.

In the fading afternoon sun, Lydia spent the next hour running from one part of the playground to the other, entertaining Julia the best she could, all under the watchful eye of her mother, observing from afar.

When Julia's eyes became heavy and her energy had

slowed, Lydia returned her to her mother. The young woman couldn't express her gratitude as Lydia took Yankee and exchanged pleasantries. Before Lydia left, she asked, "I own the bookshop across the street. I'd love to share a wonderful children's book with her. Do you mind waiting a few minutes, and I'll run over and get it?"

Sweat trickled across the woman's brow as she tried to accept Lydia's offer gracefully. "Good. Stay right here. I'll be right back."

When Lydia returned from retrieving the book, her heart sank when Julia and her mother were nowhere to be found. She scanned the park, and a stab of disappointment twisted as she clutched the book in her hands.

Sitting on the bench, she sighed a heavy groan as the weight of her troubles bore down on her again—a longing stirred within her during their brief encounter. For a few fleeting moments, she had a connection to the child, a glimpse of the motherhood she gave away. She couldn't help but wonder what her daughter was doing at that moment, or for that matter, where she might be.

Lydia didn't know how long she sat on the bench alone, but as her eyes started to wane, she mustered enough energy to return home alone and more distressed than when she'd come.

***

There was no denying Mattie Rose's anguish as her bottom lip trembled as she begged to visit Lydia. "Please, *Datt*."

Aaron heaved a sigh, torn between his emotions and his daughter's discomfort. "Lydia is busy these days, and I'm not sure she would welcome an unexpected visit from us."

As they approached the bookshop, Aaron felt himself grow anxious. He couldn't shake the memory of his last visit with Lydia, and as he became quiet, Mattie Rose could hardly contain her excitement. After setting the foot brake of his buggy, he lifted Mattie Rose down from the bench seat and let her run off to the store's entrance.

Upon entering the store, Aaron tried to avoid meeting Lydia's eyes straight on and followed Mattie Rose to the kids' corner of the shop without saying hello.

Lydia broke the silence by moving to Mattie Roses's side to help her find the next book in the series she was enjoying. "It's so good to see you." Lydia patted the top of the little girl's head. "How's my favorite five-year-old?"

"Almost…" Mattie Rose held up six fingers.

"That's right, you'll be six next week. What are you going to do for your big day?"

Mattie shrugged her shoulders, looked up at Aaron, and hopefully asked, "Party?"

He hadn't thought about her birthday beyond next week and didn't know how to answer his daughter's pleading blue eyes. "Is that what you want?"

Mattie Rose wrapped her arms around Lydia's waist and looked up at her. "You'll come?"

Aaron and Lydia exchanged guarded glances before she replied, "If it's alright with your *datt*, I'd love to."

Aaron felt his body stiffen, but he nodded instead of answering, fearing his tone would reveal the true condition of his heart at that moment. Pointing to the shelf of books, he added, "I need to talk to Lydia for a few minutes. Go ahead and pick out a couple of books."

Aaron guided Lydia back toward the counter as he muttered, "I need to talk to you about something."

Lydia grabbed a stack of magazines to straighten and asked, "What is it?"

Words always came, but at that moment, he struggled to

convey the severity of what he'd been hearing throughout the community. He took a long breath before continuing. "The bishop has heard about the changes you're making to the bookshop." He paused for a moment to watch her reaction before adding. "There are rumors that he's warning those with young children to keep them from spending too much time here for fear of the worldly influences you are initiating."

Lydia's shoulders sank, and he was quick to add. "I'm sorry, Lydia. I know how much the store means to you, but I felt obligated to tell you what's happening."

"It isn't anything I didn't think would cause some stir among the People but to keep the children from visiting the bookshop," Lydia said, shaking her head in disbelief. "I'm afraid of what that might mean for teenagers. They're already limited to the type of entertainment they can partake in. Won't this force them to look for fun elsewhere?"

Aaron stiffened at her questions that hinted at her past, and he couldn't help but respond. "You had the bookshop to immerse yourself into, and you still wandered away."

"Exactly." She replied harshly. "Whether I bring the Internet into the shop has little relevance to what one might choose to do."

Aaron replied, his forehead showing signs of worry. "Regardless, the bishop's concerns are valid, and I'm starting to wonder if maybe he's right."

"So, you think I'm going to lead our community astray with a few modern conveniences?"

Aaron's jaw tightened as he thought for a second before he said something he couldn't take back. "Perhaps you've spent too much time in the world to know what's best for the young people in our community."

Lydia's face turned sour as she asked, "What are you trying to say?"

Aaron shook his head, his expression pained as he persisted, "I'm trying to say I'm afraid of the influence you might have on Mattie Rose. She's impressionable and missing her *mamm*. I, for one, don't want her exposed to things that could pull her away from our way of life."

Lydia tilted in and hissed through gritted teeth. "I would never interfere with your parenting." It was clear to Aaron that she was struggling to contain her emotions, but she continued, "But when it comes down to it, you'll need to let her forge her own path when that time comes."

Aaron hated the thoughts that were invading his mind and

could hardly contain his words as he lashed out at her by muttering, "I stood back and watched you ruin your life. I'll not do the same with my daughter."

"That's just it, Aaron… nothing you could have said or done could have changed the fact that I had to make my own mistakes, and it will be the same with Mattie Rose when she gets older."

Aaron glanced at Mattie Rose before adding, "I think she shouldn't get too attached to you or this place."

"So what? You're saying you don't want her to see me anymore? To spend time with me?"

There were no words he could say to ease the pain etched on Lydia's face, so he gave her a quick nod and called Mattie Rose over to pay for her book.

Mattie Rose's footsteps approached, her small figure bouncing eagerly over the tense atmosphere.

"What's wrong, *Datt*?"

Aaron's heart sank as he realized she picked up on the strained conversation. He exchanged a quick glance with Lydia and answered, "It's nothing, we were just talking about the bookshop."

Mattie Rose's lips started to quiver as she looked between

the two of them. "No friends?"

Lydia knelt beside her. "Yes, dear, your *datt* and I are still friends, but sometimes friends disagree; this is one of those times."

Lydia's explanation seemed to settle her fears, and she asked, "Birthday party?"

Aaron had forgotten about her birthday party invitation and quickly laid money on the counter and replied, "I'm sure Lydia will be too busy with the store to come to your party."

With a submissive sigh, the little girl nodded, though the hurt lingered in her eyes as Aaron guided her out of the shop.

***

Lydia sank on the stool and stared at Aaron as he walked across the street to his buggy. His somber strides left her feeling raw as sadness lingered in the air.

Alone in the quiet bookshop, she tried to push the thoughts of uncertainty from her mind. She couldn't understand how Aaron could believe she would influence Mattie Rose in any manner that would be against their teachings.

As she was behind the counter, her mind drifted back to the

days of her past, when she had been consumed by grief and regret. The memories threatened to draw her back into the depths of despair. Without Ruthie's impromptu visit, she may have stayed wallowing in the darkness.

Ruthie's arrival was like a little ray of sunshine breaking through the hovering storm clouds, and Lydia couldn't help but feel a surge of hope in her cheerful voice.

It took only a few seconds for Ruthie to surmise something was amiss. "What's that forlorn look on your face? It looks like you could burst out in tears any moment."

Lydia sighed. "It's been a difficult day. Aaron and I disagreed about Mattie Rose."

"Oh no... what happened?"

Lydia recounted her conversation with Aaron and the warning the bishop was spreading around the community.

Ruthie clucked her tongue. "That's just plain foolishness!"

A bitter laugh escaped Lydia's lips. "They're convinced I'll encourage their young to jump the fence to a path of sin and discord."

Ruthie chuckled. "Goodness Lydia, you're running a bookshop, not a den of wickedness." Ruthie reached across the counter and patted the back of her hand. "I wouldn't worry too much. Aaron will come around... you mark my word."

Lydia smiled warmly at her friend's confidence in the middle of adversity.

Ruthie crossed her arms over her chest and thought briefly before adding. "I know our community can be set in their ways, but sometimes it just takes a little persuasion to get them to see things differently."

Lydia put her elbows on the table and rested her chin in her propped-up palms. "I'm not the most popular person around these days, and I highly doubt the bishop will be open to hearing anything I might have to say."

Ruthie leaned in as if she were afraid someone would overhear their conversation even though no one was in the shop. "Nonsense! You're Wally Troyer's daughter, which holds some clout in this town."

Lydia waved off Ruthie's comment. "I doubt that. I lost that right years ago."

"I wouldn't be so quick to dismiss a visit to the bishop if you explain things and ask him to help you devise a compromise. Maybe if you offer to put some filters in place to prevent misuse, he might come around to your way of thinking."

"That might work," Lydia added. "But it still doesn't solve Aaron's issue with me spending time with Mattie Rose."

Ruthie stood and declared boldly. "That, my dear, is going to require a bit of finesse and creativity. I suggest you show up to her birthday uninvited."

"Oh my! I couldn't do that. He made it quite clear I wasn't welcome."

Ruthie threw her hands up in the air. "Hogwash! Then you go and re-invite yourself. I'd say Aaron needs a little reminder of how much you mean to Mattie Rose, and besides, it's her birthday, not his."

Lydia took a deep breath. "I don't know. What if I upset him?"

"I have a feeling that once Mattie Rose sees you, and Aaron realizes how happy she is that you're there, he won't stay mad for long."

***

A few days later, Lydia parked her car at the end of the driveway and walked past the row of buggies lined up near Aaron's porch. As she ascended the stairs, she heard laughter and chatter inside the house. Taking a concentrated breath, she knocked on the door.

Aaron's smile faded as he rounded the corner and saw her on the other side of the screen door.

"I, uh, I brought a present for Mattie Rose." She replied as she held out a pink gift bag.

They stood awkwardly for a moment, the sounds of the party drifting out from behind Aaron. Finally, Lydia spoke up. "Can we talk?"

Aaron pushed onto the porch, leading her to follow him to the far end. They sat in silence for a few seconds before Lydia spoke up again. "I was hoping we could put our differences aside for today and celebrate Mattie Rose's birthday together," she said softly.

Aaron took the present from Lydia's hand and stood. "Thank you," he replied in a hesitant tendency. "I'm sure she'll appreciate it."

As she viewed him move back toward the door, she was still uncertain if he would agree to her presence at the celebration. He stopped at the door and held it open silently for her to enter. She hesitated momentarily, searching his eyes for any hint of what he might be hiding behind his thoughtful glare.

Lydia couldn't resist breaking the uneasy silence. "Thank you," she murmured quietly.

His face softened at her sincerity. "I'm glad you came," he whispered even though his tone still held a hint of reservation.

With a small nod, she marched into his house as Mattie Rose ran to her side and engulfed her in a tender hug. "My birthday wish came true," Mattie Rose exclaimed.

Over the sudden burst of noise, Lydia looked back at Aaron whose eyes held a mixture of warmth and longing. Caught off guard by the vulnerability, Lydia's heart skipped a beat as their eyes locked in the silent exchange.

With Mattie Rose still clinging to her, Lydia found herself unable to break free from Aaron's steady gaze. For a moment, it seemed as if the walls between them had crumbled, leaving a path of raw emotions in its path.

She had to swallow hard at the sudden warmth spreading across his face. But it disappeared as quickly as it played out, leaving her with a deeper sense of rejection and emptiness.

Tracy Fredrychowski

CHAPTER 13

Sweat trickled down Aaron's face as he stacked hay in the barn. Memories of Lydia's surprise visit the night before still hung in the air as he tried to put her out of his mind.

As the hot afternoon sun filtered between the cracks of the old barn, a shadow fell across the doorway, and he turned to see Jimmy Scott. Aaron's stomach twisted as he tipped his chin to the unwelcome visitor. "To what do I owe the displeasure of your visit?"

Jimmy sneered in response. "Just thought I'd pay an old friend a visit."

Aaron positioned the last bale of straw in the stack and scoffed. "I wouldn't go that far."

"Come on, man, if we shared a woman, we have more in common than you give us credit for."

Jimmy's smirk sent a chill down the back of Aaron's neck, and he rested long enough to wipe the sweat from his brow before responding. "I'm busy... what do you want?"

Jimmy rested his foot on an overturned bucket and picked up a piece of straw to balance between his teeth. "I suppose I came to offer a friendly warning."

Aaron pulled the bucket out from under Jimmy's foot and spat. "If you've got something to say, just spit it out and be done with it."

Jimmy composed his posture and circled around Aaron like a vulture closing in on his prey. "I've seen you with Lydia, and I've come to stake my claim on what's rightfully mine."

Aaron chortled. "I hardly think you have any right to her," he took a step back. "The last I knew, she pretty much despises you."

Jimmy moved so close that Aaron could smell stale beer on his breath as he mocked a reply. "I suppose it's all in what you can read between the lines, and in my books, I have little Miss Lydia Troyer right where I want her."

Aaron squared his shoulders and stood his ground. "What makes you think she wants anything to do with you?"

Jimmy grunted. "Because Mr. All and Mighty, I hold a piece of her you'll never have. The part she gave away that binds her to me forever... I hold a piece of her past she'll never share with you." Jimmy leaned in close, his breath hot against Aaron's ear. "You might think you know her, but you have no idea what she's capable of. Trust me, you'd be wise to stay clear of her once and for all." Jimmy turned to leave but hollered a final warning over his shoulder on his way out. "It'd be in your best interest to encourage her to sell that dilapidated building and get herself back to Pittsburgh where she belongs."

It took Aaron a few minutes to process Jimmy's sickening words and a little longer to understand their twisted meaning. Both confused the daylight out of him, so much so the sinking feeling swirling around his head forced him to drop what he was doing to warn Lydia of Jimmy's visit.

***

Lydia took advantage of the quiet afternoon to delve deeper into her father's journals. She wasn't sure what she was looking for, but ever since they had located the passageways, there was something disturbing about the way her father's entries seemed to hint about something more than what they could see on the surface.

The pages revealed snippets of conversations that didn't

make sense until then. The more she read, the more she started to put the pieces together of the cryptic clues he had left her to discover. It was apparent her father had stumbled upon something dangerous, and she couldn't help but sense it led to his untimely death.

Among the tangled threads of information, she found references to a meeting dating back almost five years. Scribbled in the corner of one of the pages were the initials SP&MM and a large, circled question mark. Her father noted that he was at the Sandwich Shoppe taking specific notes of the people who sat around him that day. Most were Willow Springs, Main Street merchants.

Her heart raced, trying to understand why that day seemed so important to her... and then it dawned on her it was the exact day she had left her goodbye in the cash register. She had been watching the store that morning as he sat next door enjoying a cup of coffee.

Lydia closed the journal just as the door of the bookshop squeaked open. Detective Powers stepped inside and took a second to remove his sunglasses and adjust his eyes to the difference in light. "Busy?" he asked.

Lydia waved her hand out over the empty store. "Not much

business these days."

"A summer lull?" he inquired.

Lydia sighed. "No, more like a bishop-instated boycott."

Detective Powers nodded. "I see… that stinks," he added.

"I'm glad you stopped in. I have some interesting things to show you." Lydia opened the journal. "Some of my father's entries are most peculiar." She flipped to one of the early records. "He's listed many dates, newspapers, and a few names." She turned the book toward him. "Do you recognize any of these names?"

"I do. Some of these people are powerful outside of Willow Springs." The detective snapped a picture of the journal entry. "It'll be interesting to see what connection any of these people have to Willow Springs."

Lydia held the pages flat while he snapped a few more shots of other pages she pointed out. "I was going to start looking up some of those dates and newspapers, but I need to go to the library to do that," Lydia mentioned. "I have the uncanny belief that my father was trying to piece something together."

Detective Powers took a seat on the stool next to the counter. "Those articles and names might hold the key to this puzzle, and it might tell us what your father was tracking."

Lydia ran a loving finger over her father's writing. "I can't help but think he got too close to something. Particularly since you think he was poisoned." Lydia closed the book. "But why would these men be interested in Willow Springs? There's not much here but a bunch of hard-working people with little to offer."

"That's where you're wrong," he stated. "An Amish community is the perfect cover for illegal trafficking. First, they're not likely to run to the police when they see something unusual, and second, no one would think twice about using those underground passages to smuggle drugs in and out of Pittsburgh."

"So now what?" she asked.

"We keep digging until I find a connection between those names and those articles."

The quietness of the shop left them both lost in their thoughts before the detective asked, "So, you called and left a message for me to stop by today. Was this what you wanted to talk about?"

"Oh my, no, I almost forgot. It's my father's collection of old books. Two more editions have come up missing."

"Since you moved them upstairs?"

"Yes. I haven't noticed anything else missing, just two of the most valuable books."

The detective took out his notebook and started jotting down the details. Lydia rattled off the titles, and he asked what the antique books looked like as he continued to question her. "Did anyone have access or know about you moving them besides yourself?"

"You and Aaron."

"Have you entertained any visitors since moving them upstairs?"

Lydia hesitated for a moment before responding to Detective Powers' question. "Well, one person visited," she admitted reluctantly. "My brother, Harvey, was in my apartment last week."

The detective raised an eyebrow. "Your brother, huh? Did he have any reason to take them?"

Lydia shook her head, her mind racing with possibilities. "I'm not sure," she admitted. "But it might be worth me asking him. Do you mind if I ask him before I file a report?"

"Sure, I have enough to do with tracing down this list of names to keep me busy for the rest of the day."

The knot forming in Lydia's throat pained her as she

contemplated having to face Harvey head-on and uncover the reason behind the truth, no matter the cost.

***

Knowing the exact time her *bruders* broke for dinner each day, Lydia parked her car at the end of the lane and walked to Harvey's office through the back field and into the empty barn.

As she quietly sifted through his office, looking for anything to help her understand his motives, she sifted through stacks of invoices and bank statements. Pulling the desk drawer open, she pressed aside a half-opened pipe tobacco pouch, leaving the scent of cherry wood along its path. The scent invoked a memory of her father she had to block as she dug deeper into Harvey's private space.

Suddenly, footsteps approaching the door sent a jolt of fear through her body, forcing her to crouch to the floor and crawl under the desk.

The door creaked open, and Harvey's voice packed the room. "Unless you have something good to report, I don't have time for your excuses."

Ed Glick's speech took on a condescending air. "You'd

better make time if you know what's good for you. The boss is getting impatient and wants those books delivered ASAP."

Lydia's breath caught in her throat as she strained to keep from moving and stay hidden.

Harvey's voice took on a note of frustration. "Like I told you before, I'm not handing over any more until I see the replicas and get paid for those we've already delivered. There's too much at stake, and I'm tired of playing games."

Lydia noted Harvey's footsteps as he moved to the file cabinet by the door, pushing Ed aside as he opened the drawer. "Now, if you want to take that information back to him, so be it, but I'm not supplying another thing, and I've run out of options."

Ed scoffed. "You always have options."

"Not this time. My *schwester* is headstrong and won't be persuaded to sell the shop. These books are my last chance to settle things."

Harvery's voice lowered, thick with an edge of anger. "I'm telling you; it won't take her long to realize the value of the old man's collection. And once she does, she'll figure out many of the books are fakes. She's not stupid for sure and certain…"

Ed interrupted. "Neither of us can afford for that to happen.

She's seen me here, and it won't take her long to put two and two together to make a whole heap of trouble for the both of us."

Lydia could hardly believe her ears. She couldn't imagine what kind of financial trouble Harvey had that he would resort to stealing from his father. Her own *bruder* conspiring with the likes of Ed Glick made her skin crawl.

She waited until their voices carried outside before she snuck out the back of the barn and back to her hidden car.

***

An approaching buggy alerted Aaron to the bishop's visit, and he walked out to the front porch to greet him. His stomach churned as he witnessed the stern countenance across the old man's brow.

"Good afternoon, Mose," Aaron said cordially, even though he sensed his visit would be anything but friendly. "To what do I owe the honor of your visit?"

The bishop stayed seated in the open buggy, so Aaron walked to his side, taking note of how the man's demeanor changed the closer he got. "Aaron, I've heard troubling rumors about your association with Lydia Troyer," he began, his voice commanding authority.

Suddenly, Aaron understood the reason for his bishop to visit. "I assure you it's nothing more than friendship and honoring the work I'd started for Wally before his passing."

The bishop's words grew sharper. "I don't need to remind you of your church membership and your promise to follow the *Ordnung*." Aaron's mouth dried as bile rose in his throat. He had to swallow hard as the bishop continued. "I cannot condone your involvement with someone who has turned her back on our way of life and has put the welfare of our young people in jeopardy."

Aaron struggled to maintain his composure in the face of the bishop's condemnation. "With all due respect, Lydia is still a member of this community, Amish or *Englisch*. She lives in Willow Springs and is our neighbor," he argued.

The bishop picked up the reins and offered a final warning. "I urge you to reconsider your alliance. You must choose where your loyalties lie—with the Old Order or those seeking to undermine our traditions."

As Aaron observed the bishop pull away, he wondered if his relationship with Lydia was doomed if he continued on his current path. It wasn't the first time he challenged his loyalty to the Old Order over the last few years. He often pondered the possibility of seeking church membership at the more liberal New Order Fellowship.

***

The streetlight flickered on as Lydia walked briskly along the deserted sidewalk outside the library. The warm summer evening left her t-shirt clinging to her skin, adding a sense of discomfort to an already challenging day.

Passing by the dimly lit alleyway gave her cause to quicken her steps. Out of the corner of her eye, she glimpsed the shadow of a figure lurking in the darkness as if he were watching her.

The pounding in her ears replicated the beating of her heart as she crossed the street. Following the light to the Sandwich Shoppe, she quickly stepped inside the café, seeking a temporary reprieve from her overactive imagination. After ordering a coffee, she sat in the corner and let the comforting aroma of freshly brewed coffee calm her. The late-night chatter was a warm welcome, but she still couldn't shake the feeling of apprehension.

Eventually, she reluctantly left the Sandwich Shoppe and made her way home. As she approached, the lock appeared to have been tampered with, forcing the air from her lungs as she pushed it open cautiously, her senses on high alert.

The counter had been ransacked. Drawers were pulled out, and papers were scattered across the floor. Fear creeped through Lydia as she realized someone had been inside the bookshop while she was at the library.

An unsettling chaos hovered in the air, and she made her way to her apartment to find it worse. Furniture had been overturned, and her father's chair slashed, leaving pieces of foam scattered over the floor. A small gasp escaped her lips when she saw the knife stuck in the middle of the island with a note pinned to the butcher block. STAY OUT OF THINGS YOU DON'T UNDERSTAND. YOU'RE IN OVER YOUR HEAD.

Heart pounding, she dialed Detective Powers.

***

Lydia glanced up from her desk as Aaron entered the bookshop, a wave of relief washing over her at the sight of his

215

familiar face.

Aaron hesitated; his expression troubled as he walked closer. "Lewis paid me a visit this morning." He took off his straw hat and stood at the counter. "I wanted to check on you."

Fighting to control the lump forming in her throat, Lydia whispered, "*Jah*. It was unnerving, to say the least. But I feel much better this morning."

Aaron twirled his hat between his fingertips. "Maybe it would be best if you stayed with one of your *bruders* for a while until Lewis gets to the bottom of all this."

Lydia sighed, resting her chin in the palm of her hand. "I can't just walk away. If I do, whoever is trying to scare me will win."

After everything they'd gone through the last couple of weeks, Lydia couldn't help but notice the genuine concern evident on Aaron's face. "I'm sorry I've pulled you into all this," she mumbled.

"There's no need to worry about me. I can take care of myself, and I'm not easily intimidated by all the unexpected visitors I've been receiving. But you need to consider your safety," he urged gently.

A pang of guilt washed over Lydia as she realized how her

actions must also affect Aaron. "Visitors?"

Aaron chuckled. "*Jah*, but again, you don't worry about any of that. I've learned to take much of what people say with a grain of salt."

"I'm sorry," she whispered.

Aaron nervously shifted from foot to foot before stating, "Jimmy Scott stopped by yesterday to have a friendly chat with me."

"Friendly chat? I'm not sure he has that in him." Lydia lifted her chin. "What did he want to talk about?"

"Our mutual interest."

Confusion settled across her forehead. "Me?"

Aaron nodded. "Seems he stopped to warn me of your wicked ways and to stake his claim on you."

Lydia let out a long moan. "Claim on me!" she ran her hands through her hair, "There isn't an ounce of me that would ever consider entangling myself with the likes of him again. I learned my lesson the hard way with him. His only significance is in proving himself to his overbearing father and securing the integrity of his family's name."

Aaron stepped closer and muttered, "He insinuated a few things that left me wondering if he has ulterior motives for trying to secure a place in your life again."

Lydia nodded solemnly and asked, "What did he say?"

In a severe tone, Aaron inserted, "Perhaps that's a conversation for another time." He replaced his straw hat and continued, "Please, promise me you'll be careful."

How Aaron sidestepped her question left Lydia with an overwhelming sense of dread at what Jimmy may have told Aaron. "I won't let fear, or some mindless threats force me to leave my father's dream."

Aaron turned to leave but stopped abruptly and asked, "But is it your dream?"

CHAPTER 14

Lydia sat across from Detective Powers as the late afternoon sun lingered rays just beyond the horizon, shining rays through the parted blinds in the cluttered office.

The detective leaned back in his chair, sending a squeak echoing through the small room. "I've been connecting the dots between the list of names you found, and I've come up with a few interesting connections."

Lydia crossed her legs and balanced her elbows on her knee, leaning forward in anticipation of his discovery. "Like what?" she asked curiously.

"Every person on the list has a connection in one way or another with Markle Media and or Scott Properties."

"What is their connection?"

"Money, property, and business transactions that haven't been easy to trace," Lewis stated. "And it seems there's more to their involvement than meets the eye."

"What have you uncovered?"

Detective Powers tapped his pencil on one of the documents before him. "Turns out that Ben Markle's and Jimmy Scott's fathers were college roommates," he revealed, his words lingering with suspicion. "Scott Properties stands to gain a lot if they can secure Main Street."

Lydia shook her head, trying to make sense of the connection. "So, you think Ben is working with Scott Properties?" She rested back in her chair and lingered, adding, "Markle has made it clear he wanted to help me sell the store."

"I think his part in all this goes deeper than you can even imagine," the detective added. "Lydia, I have to ask you some questions about your past and connection to Jimmy Scott."

Lydia breathed and nodded grimly.

He leaned back in his chair again, deep in thought. "I think you've played a bigger role in their plans than you realize," the detective's brow moved in concentration as he continued, "Perhaps there's something about you or your father that they were counting on to further their agenda."

Lydia shook her head, feeling a knot of frustration lodged in her chest. "But why would they involve me in their plans?" she wondered aloud.

"In cases like this and specifically with the men on that list, a plan like this takes years to orchestrate, and it often involves innocent people who have no idea they've been used to carry out their well-thought-out plans."

"My father was just a hard-working Amish man. What could they possibly want from him?"

"Property. He held the keys to one of the most historic buildings in Willow Springs, and they needed to gain access to it regardless of the cost to him or his family."

"And you think they included me in their plans somehow?"

"I do. That's why I must ask you how you got a job at Markle Media and your connection to Jimmy Scott."

Lydia shifted in her chair, closed her eyes, and rubbed her temples before answering. "I've tried to block much of that from my memory," she took a minute to gather her thoughts. "It was a dark time and one I don't like to talk about."

"I'm sorry, Lydia, but I think your past has somehow played a role in this." He gave her a few more seconds before he asked, "Let's start with Jimmy. How involved were you with him?"

"I had just started my *Rumspringa*. Jimmy hung out at the Sandwich Shoppe and started paying attention to me. He was older, and I must admit, it was exciting that an *Englisch* boy was talking to me at the time." Lewis didn't rush her, and it took her a few minutes to dig deep into her memory to hash out those adventurous years of her youth. "I was stepping out with Aaron at the time, but he wasn't happy I was spending so much time with my new *Englisch* friends." Regret settled over her as she recalled how upset Aaron was with her then, and it took her a few minutes to regain her voice so she could continue. "My father and *bruders* were beside themselves. The more they pressed, the further I stepped over the fence. It wasn't long before I was sneaking out at night to meet Jimmy, and we'd drive all over town in his Camaro."

"The same car he drives today?" Lewis asked.

"Yes, it was his pride and joy. If I remember correctly, he once mentioned that his father gave it to him in exchange for a job he wanted Jimmy to work on."

"Do you know what that job was?"

Lydia shook her head. "Can't say I do. He may have told me, but I don't remember. He was proud of it and said he'd do whatever it took to keep it."

The detective wrote down a few notes and continued to ask her another question. "Tell me how you ended up in Pittsburgh."

Lydia's heart pounded, and she felt tears welling up, which she forced away before answering. "I couldn't stay here. I had disgraced myself and my family, and the thought of facing my father was more than I could bear. When Jimmy suggested we move, I let him convince me to move to Pittsburgh with him. At the time, I thought he would marry me once he found out about... the baby."

Lydia couldn't look the detective in the face. Instead, she looked to the floor to admit more of her shame. "He got scared and left me on the steps of a woman's shelter."

"And the baby?" he asked.

"I gave her up." Her voice cracked as she muttered, "I had no choice. I was too embarrassed to go home and afraid to raise her by myself."

The detective let the air settle for a few minutes before probing her again. "And your job at Markle Media. How did that come about?"

"That was the strangest thing. I had barely finished getting my GED when I got a call telling me that someone from the school had set up an interview for a reception position there."

"Interesting. And how were your interactions with Ben Markle?"

"Odd, to say the least. Almost creepy. He paid too much attention to me, and I'm pretty sure he had a lot to do with me getting the podcast interviewer job."

"How about after you moved back to Willow Springs?"

"He's paid me more than one visit, hoping to convince me to return and work for him. And, like I said, he's offered to help me get out from underneath the bookshop."

"Lydia, I have a sense you've been used as a pawn in obtaining your father's building. And I think it goes as far back as Jimmy. I can't put my finger on it yet, but I bet he got that car in exchange for securing a relationship with you. What he didn't count on was a pregnancy."

"Jimmy was so upset and begged me not to go to his father about the baby. He was sure his father would disown him, and he would lose his inheritance if he found out what he'd done."

Detective Powers folded his arms across his chest. "Lose his inheritance over a child?"

"If I remember correctly, his father was born out of wedlock and constantly threatened Jimmy with not tarnishing their family name."

Lewis interrupted, "So his father knew about your relationship?"

She crunched up her shoulders. "I'm not sure. As I look back on it, I think Jimmy just used me to prove something to his father. It wasn't until… until…" she swallowed hard, unable to share the truth so forthright, "until he forced himself on me that I realized I was nothing more than a passing fancy to him. He played along for another few months until I told him I was pregnant."

"I'm sorry you had to get mixed up with the likes of him," he said softly.

"But what about my father? How does he fit into all this?" Lydia asked.

"I think he got too close to the truth. Can you think of anything in your father's journal that would give us more clues about what he was on to?"

Lydia reached into her purse, pulled out a photo, and thrust it across the desk. "That's my daughter and her adoptive family. My father knew about the baby."

"How can you be so sure?"

"That quilt was mine, and I wrapped my baby in it when I handed her over… he would have recognized it."

Silence covered the air between them as Detective Powers remained deep in thought for a few minutes, allowing Lydia to compose herself.

"I know this may sound unconventional, but hear me out," he began slow and steady. "There's so much more to your involvement in this scheme, and I think we can use you to get Jimmy to let you in on his plans... that is, if you agree." He stopped, waited, and continued when she didn't say anything immediately. "His family has deep connections from here to Pittsburgh, and I believe Scott Properties is a major player. If we can get you walking in their inner circles, you might be able to gather information about what's going on behind the scenes."

Every part of Lydia's body recoiled with the thought of letting Jimmy get close to her again, but she couldn't deny the potential benefits of having an inside source, especially if it meant she could find out if they had anything to do with her father's death.

"How do you propose I do that?" she asked, her pitch skeptical. "He knows I can't stand the air he breathes."

"I think you just need to encourage him a little. He's so arrogant he'll take an ounce and run with it, particularly after his conversation with Aaron. He's out to prove you can't be trusted to Aaron." He bent forward, his look serious. "You'll have to tread carefully, and we can't let anyone suspect that you're working with us. Not even Aaron."

"Alright," she said in a manner that conveyed the heaviness of what he was asking her to do. "I'll do it, but I have to be careful not to put myself in a position where he can manipulate me again."

Detective Powers gave her a nod of approval. "Good. We'll proceed cautiously, and I'll ensure you're safe wherever you go. He's not to be trusted."

Lydia's stomach twisted in apprehension, but she knew if she wanted to protect her town and her family, she'd have to put herself in the line of fire for a short time. She only prayed Aaron would understand and forgive her when it was all over.

***

As Lydia arranged an order of new books on the bookshelf, she glanced up to see Jimmy sauntering in, making himself known most obnoxiously. A wave of nausea fluttered through her stomach before putting on a forced grin to greet him.

"Still trying to make a go of this place?" He said, his pitch lifting in disgust. "How long will you keep yourself stuck in the town, huh?"

Taking in a silent breath, she moaned out a believable lie. "Just trying to make the best of it."

Jimmy chuckled, leaning on the corner of the large bookshelf. "You deserve better than this place. You always did." He looked around the aging shop, with a lack of paying customers, and inserted, "You shouldn't have come back here. There's so much more to life than this."

Her pulse quickened as she led him into the trap she was trying to set. "I've been thinking the same thing," she admitted, her nature carefully casual. "This town, these rules... they're suffocating."

The smile that spread across his face was exactly what she had planned for, and he bowed in and sneered, "Then leave with me. Let's sell this place and move back to Pittsburgh. With the money you make, you could start all over..." he wrapped his arm around her waist and pulled her close, "we could start over."

She found herself nodding along with Jimmy's persuasive words, knowing she was treading on dangerous territory, but before she gave him too much too fast, she pulled away. "I can't just leave like that. I have responsibilities. I'm not sure I'm ready to trust you again."

Not letting her go, he held her tighter and whispered, "Now, I wasn't that bad, was I?"

His hot breath made her skin crawl, and she closed her eyes, hoping to endure his closeness. When he loosened his grip, she opened her eyes and saw movement just outside the bookshop window. Her heart sank when she saw Aaron standing just beyond the glass, his expression unreadable as he scrutinized them. With a heavy heart, she knew she had to make Aaron believe she was turning her attention to Jimmy, even though every fiber of her being screamed otherwise.

She twisted closer, shut her eyes, and allowed herself to be enveloped by his charm while being aware of Aaron's piercing stare boring into her from outside.

She turned so her back was to the window, forcing herself to maintain the façade for Aaron's sake, knowing that her true intentions had to remain hidden, even if it meant breaking his heart in the process.

***

Aaron approached the bookshop, his heart pounding with a mixture of nerves and determination. He finally decided to tell

Lydia how he felt, to be honest with what he'd been fighting since she returned to Willow Springs.

Walking across the street, he detected the red Camaro parked in front of the shop, and quickened his steps. As he neared the front of the shop, he slowed when he caught sight of Lydia through the window. A knot of jealousy and fear wrung his gut. The thought of losing her to the outside world again landed heavily on his shoulders, forcing him to clench his fists at his sides.

He refused to let history repeat itself and shoved aside his doubts and fears, focusing instead on how he could keep her from slipping through his fingers again.

He watched Jimmy wrap a snake-like arm around Lydia's waist, forcing him to suck in a breath as his jaw twitched, sensing Jimmy's actions were masking darker intentions. Aaron knew all too well the kind of man he was — a smooth talker with a sharp edge of deceit hidden behind fast cars and fancy clothes.

Seeing her drawn into his web of lies and heartless threats pained him. He had to find a way to warn her… to make her see the truth behind his motives. Despite the turmoil, Aaron couldn't tear himself away from the scene. He couldn't help but wonder what hold Jimmy had over her. Could it be the one thing Jimmy had waved under his nose the day before?

As the minutes stretched, he finally refused to stand idly by and watch as Jimmy Scott wormed his way back into Lydia's life. As he turned to walk away, he vowed to fight for Lydia's heart, to prove once and for all that what they once had could be restored.

***

Once Lydia realized Aaron had left his observation spot, she pulled herself away from Jimmy's embrace. "Jimmy," she began, her voice soft but firm, "I can't just up and leave Willow Springs and my father's bookshop like that. It's not that simple." She returned to stacking books and added, "While leaving this place is tempting, I don't think I want to give up so quickly, and I certainly don't want to sell the store. It's all I have."

With a hint of frustration, Jimmy added, "But look at this place. It's falling down around you, and I have a buyer just itching to get his hands on this place."

Lydia studied how he fidgeted from one foot to the other,

which he often did when he was nervous. She knew she needed to tread carefully to keep him interested without giving away too much of herself in the process.

"And just think what we could do if we got away from this town. If you're here, you'll never escape the judgment of your *bruders* and the Amish community." He moved closer and muttered close to her ear. "You're not Amish anymore, and you'll never be accepted here like you once were. Why would you want to stay here?"

Lydia forced a smile, even though she knew part of what he was saying was true. Regardless of his claims, she couldn't be swayed from their plan. "I understand what you're saying, but I'm not ready to give all this up yet."

As she spoke, she couldn't shake the concern she was playing right into a trap about ready to swallow her whole. But she also knew she had to keep him at arm's length to protect herself and everything she held dear.

"Lydia," Jimmy began, his tone shifting, "you know I can't stay in this small town. There's nothing here for me, and besides, my job is in Pittsburgh."

Despite his rising voice, Lydia tried to maintain her composure, keeping the air void of the turmoil inside. She knew she was playing a dangerous game of allure that might come back to bite her if she wasn't careful.

"Perhaps," she replied, "if you gave Willow Springs a chance, we could revisit what we once had." She moved closer and laid her hand on his arm. "Who knows what the future might hold?" She examined as his eyes softened at the spot where his brow met his forehead, a glimmer of hope flickering in his eyes.

Jimmy planted a kiss on Lydia's cheek and turned to leave, all while a sly grin played on the corner of his lips. His mind was already spinning at her sudden change of heart, but he wasn't one to trust quickly. No, he knew better than to believe her recent actions lined up fully with their brief encounter.

As he strode onto Main Street, the busy town seemed to close in, suffocating him with its backwardness. The scent of fresh horse dung occupied his nostrils, only fueling his frustrations. With Lydia's voice still ringing in his ears, he swore he'd play her little game, but he was no stranger to manipulation. He would gladly lead if she wanted to dance, but he'd do it on his own terms. Perhaps this time, he could take more than her virtue. He could take back what was rightfully his—the power, control, the satisfaction of knowing he had beaten her at her own game.

CHAPTER 15

An eerie heaviness covered Lydia for the rest of the day, and it took all she had to block the image of Aaron's face from her mind as she went about her duties at the bookshop. After stepping next door to order a sandwich, she brought it back and settled at the counter for supper. Her heart quickened when she heard a faint groan from the floorboards in her apartment above.

Without hesitation, she quietly headed upstairs, Yankee on her heels. The hair on the back of her neck stood on end as she reached for the doorknob, her heart pounding. She slowly pushed the door open to the dimly lit room with a trembling hand.

As the door creaked open, a chill swept through the room, and Yankee let out a low growl, leaving the air thick with tension. Suddenly, a shadow moved in the corner of the room, and Yankee let go of a whole bark.

"Who's there?" she called out, her voice barely above a whisper. But there was no response, only the sound of her own ragged breathing.

Summoning all the courage she could muster, she pressed on, her senses on full alert. With each step, the hunch of dread intensified, and she felt the manifestation of someone coming near.

A tall, lanky figure emerged dressed all in black, causing Yankee to charge forward and Lydia to scream. She stumbled backward as he rammed past her, scrambling to put distance between herself and the intruder. His footsteps echoed off the stairway as fear coursed through Lydia's veins.

With Yankee tightly by her side, Lydia fought to find her footing and followed the figure downstairs. In the light of the bookshop, she stalked the man as he darted out the door, a book clasped tightly in his grasp. Adrenaline surged as she realized the figure looked much like Ed Glick.

Fueled by determination, she raced after him, her footsteps echoing against the wooden floorboards. She burst through the door and onto the sidewalk, the hot summer air slapping her face along the way.

"Come back here!" she yelled; her voice laden with fury.

But he was already disappearing into the shadows of the setting sun. Breathing heavily, Lydia stopped at the end of the block, watching helplessly as he vanished into the back alley of Main Street.

Aaron's buggy barely stopped before he jumped down and ran to her side. "Lydia, what's wrong? Why were you running like that?"

Breathless and shaken, Lydia tried to explain what she had just witnessed. "Someone was in my apartment. I was only gone for a few minutes. I'm almost certain it was Ed, and he had another book."

Aaron took a second to process her words. "Are you sure it was him?"

Lydia shook her head, her voice trembling. "I can't be certain, but it looked like him. I know it sounds crazy, but…"

Before she could finish her sentence, Aaron's protective instincts kicked in, his concern turning to frustration. "Lydia, what were you thinking, chasing after him like that? You could have been hurt!"

He took a deep breath, trying to settle his emotions. "It's not safe for you here. Those books must be more valuable than we realized if someone is willing to break in repeatedly to steal them."

Lydia nodded, the sound of fear settling in her voice. "I know. That's why I need to confront Harvey. He's wrapped up in this, and I need to get to the bottom of it once and for all."

"I'm not letting you face Harvey alone; we'll go together." Aaron declared.

Abruptly, Lydia regained her composure and glanced past his shoulder to the shop down the street. Jimmy had pulled up and was heading their way. Avoiding looking at him in the eye, she muttered. "*Nee*, I won't do it alone."

Aaron turned to follow Lydia's gaze. As if he'd been stabbed in the heart, he realized what she meant. The sight of Jimmy approaching them felt like the worst kind of betrayal.

In a tone he didn't recognize, she abruptly excused herself. "I need to go." She turned back briefly, with a hint of warmth in her eyes, and inserted, "Thank you for checking on me." With that, she turned on her heel and hurried away, leaving Aaron standing on the sidewalk, feeling defeated again.

***

Dark clouds rolled in as Lydia stood on the sidewalk with Jimmy. In the distance, thunder rumbled, and a swift wind picked up, swirling a few flower petals from a nearby hanging basket around them. Raindrops began to fall, as scattered droplets turned into a steady downpour as they moved back inside the bookshop.

Lydia's emotions raged amidst the storm both externally and internally. She knew she'd mistakenly refused Aaron's help, but she had to keep up the façade to protect him.

When lightning illuminated the sky and thunder boomed overhead, she hugged herself tightly, rubbed her arms, and sighed silently.

"What was he doing here?" Jimmy demanded.

"He saw me running down the street and stopped to check on me."

"And why were you running down the street?" Jimmy asked as he groaned when he wiped rain from his silk shirt.

"Someone came into the shop while I was getting a sandwich, and I chased him down the sidewalk."

Jimmy snorted a disgusted laugh. "What on earth could anyone find valuable in this place?"

Lydia bit her tongue at Jimmy's snide remark, trying to

respond calmly as she picked up her car keys. "My father has a collection of old books, and someone's been breaking in to steal them. I know who's behind it and need to confront them."

Jimmy grabbed the keys from her hand and threw them back on the counter. "Okay, where are we going?"

Lydia couldn't help her shoulders from slumping in defeat. "Harvey's"

"Oh good!" Jimmy exclaimed. "I like getting under that old goat's skin."

"Maybe I should go alone," Lydia replied.

"No. We had dinner plans, and I'm not giving that up. We'll stop there on our way."

Rain pounded against the car windows with relentless force as Jimmy pulled up to Harvey's barn office. The glow from the cinderblock building gave cause to Harvey still being inside. Anxiety beat in Lydia's chest as she turned to Jimmy, her voice taking on a sense of dread. "Jimmy, please stay in the car and wait for me. I need to talk to my brother alone."

Jimmy stubbornly shook his head. "I think not."

Lydia's heart sank at Jimmy's refusal, knowing his company would only complicate matters.

"Fine." Lydia relented with a heavy sigh. "But let me do all the talking. This is between me and Harvey."

Jimmy reached over, squeezed her hand, and said, "For now, but sooner or later, he'll need to learn to deal with both of us."

Lydia's skin began to crawl at Jimmy's declaration, and she pulled her hand away and stepped out into the rain. Shielding her head with both arms, she ran a few steps into the dairy barn.

Light fluttered across the hay-strewn floor as the familiar scent of hay and manure calmed Lydia's raging nerves. Despite her growing unease about Jimmy following her, she pressed on toward Harvey's office. Taking a deep breath, she pushed the door to Harvey's office open, bracing herself for whatever lay ahead.

As Lydia and Jimmy stood before Harvey, the tension in the air magnified as thunder bellowed above. Harvey's eyes darted between them; suspicion embedded across his brow.

"What's the meaning of this?" Harvey's voice sliced through the air as he glared at Jimmy.

Jimmy met Havery with defiance. "I'm here just in case Lydia needs help getting the truth out of you."

Lydia gasped and threw Jimmy a warning scowl. "Stop. The

both of you," Lydia advised. "He just came along for moral support. He has no business with you; I do."

"I don't trust him, Lydia, and besides, what are you doing with him again?"

Lydia felt a pang of guilt for not standing her ground with Jimmy about staying in the car, but she brushed it aside, focusing on the task at hand. "I need to ask you some questions about your relationship with Ed Glick."

Harvey leaned back in his chair and spat, "I'm not discussing anything with him here. Either he leaves, or this conversation has ended before it even starts."

With a deep sigh, Lydia turned toward Jimmy, knowing how stubborn he could be. "I appreciate you coming with me, but I think it might be best if you wait in the car," she suggested, hoping her words wouldn't provoke any resistance.

Jimmy's stance stiffened. "Why should I wait in the car?"

She tried to offer him a reassuring smile but chose to lay a tender hand on his arm instead. "I appreciate you coming, but I must talk privately with my brother." She squeezed his arm. "I promise I'll be quick, then we can go to dinner."

Jimmy hesitated, but finally, with a reluctant nod, he relented and headed back outside, letting the door slam behind him.

As soon as the door closed, Harvey's frustration boiled over. "What in the world are you thinking of bringing him back into your life? Have you lost your senses?" he commanded.

Lydia knew she needed to tread carefully, choosing her words wisely to avoid revealing too much of her involvement with Jimmy again. "It's not what it looks like," she whispered.

Harvey's voice raised an octave. "You've been down this road before. You didn't learn your lesson last time?"

"I know it's hard to understand, but please, I have my reasons. You'll need to trust me." She had to maintain her cover, even if it meant lying to Harvey.

Harvey shook his head in disgust. "What's so important you had to drive out here?"

Lydia squared her shoulders, meeting her *bruder's* stare head-on. "I know about the stolen books and your involvement with Ed Glick."

Harvey scoffed. "I have no idea what you're talking about."

"You do! Someone has been breaking into the shop, stealing books from *Datt's* collection and replacing them with replicas."

"How dare you think you can just waltz in here and accuse me about something you know nothing about?"

"I know enough to see through your lies," Lydia shot back.

Harvey's eyes narrowed. "Stay out of it, Lydia. You have no idea what you're getting yourself into."

Lydia stood firm. "I won't let you destroy everything our father worked for."

Harvey stood and slapped his hands on the desk. "What gives you the right to think you know anything? You've been gone for five years and have no idea what I've done for the old man."

Lydia didn't back down. "Then tell me, Harvey. Tell me what I've missed for you to think stealing from your own family was alright."

"I tried to reason with the stubborn man, but he wouldn't budge, so I had to do what was needed to save this farm and the livelihood of the rest of this family."

Lydia inhaled and sat down. "Come clean, Harvey. Tell me the truth about what's really going on."

Harvey crumbled back in his chair, his weathered face dropping from the pressure she forced upon him. "I got in over my head, and *Datt* wouldn't sell to help. Ed Glick offered me a way out, a chance to make some quick cash. I didn't think about the consequences."

Lydia felt a slight pang of sympathy for her aging *bruder*. "That doesn't excuse what you've done, Harvey."

Harvey's appearance softened, his action bearing down on him. "I know. I couldn't figure out any other way out of the mess I made."

"And stealing from your own father?"

Harvey rested his elbows on the desk and rubbed his temples. "I thought I had it all figured out, then you came back to claim what is rightfully yours, and my plan fell all apart." Harvey looked out the window to ensure Jimmy was still in the car and added, "You know that slime ball has ulterior motives?"

Lydia nodded. "And so do I." She blew out a breath from her lips. "The books, Harvey, what are you going to do about the books? I think it's only right you get them back."

"I can't. I've already spent the money I made trying to dig myself out of debt."

"What else can we do?" Lydia asked.

Harvey pulled a slip of paper from his desk. "This is what Jimmy's client is willing to pay for the bookshop."

"*Nee*, Harvey, I'm not selling, but I can let you have the rest of *Datt's* antique books to settle your debt as long as you keep Glick away from the shop."

Harvey nodded solemnly and added, "You know that's what he's after, don't you? He has no interest in you."

"Oh, believe me, I know exactly what he's after."

"Lydia? I don't like the sound of that." Havery replied with a hint of suspicion in his eyes.

"I know how to handle Jimmy Scott; you just keep Glick away from me and the shop, or I'll have no choice but to talk with Detective Powers." Stopping when she caught sight of her father's book on his desk, she picked it up and asked, "Why do you have this?"

"*Datt* gave it to me and told me to read it. Some silly notion that if I did, I'd realize why he'd never agree to sell."

"Did you read it?"

"Hardly! I have enough to worry about than getting caught up in the old man's ramblings about hidden tunnels."

She tucked the book under her arm, turned toward the door and warned, "Remember, I'm not a member of the Amish church, and I'll go to the police if you don't stop Glick."

***

Lydia sighed heavily as she propped her elbows on the

counter as the last few customers trickled out. The once-bustling store now seemed eerily quiet against the Amish community's disapproval of the changes she was making. Just as she was about to lock the door for the day, Ruthie approached carrying a casserole dish and a pitcher of meadow tea.

"Hey there, Lydia!" Ruthie called out cheerfully as she advanced through the door, the scent of something wonderful wafting in with her. "I brought us dinner. I thought maybe we could sit on the cellar patio."

A smile turned Lydia's lips as she greeted her one and only friend she had left in Willow Springs. "It sure beats peanut butter spread and day-old bread."

Ruthie bustled past her, hollering over her shoulder as she headed downstairs and out on the back porch. "Grab silverware and glasses. Come on, Yankee," she instructed as she bounced down the steps.

Ruthie set the things down and waited for Lydia to join her before she asked, "Rough day?"

Lydia nodded wearily. "You could say that. The whole town seems to be boycotting me."

"Tsk!" Ruthie snarled. "Well, what do you expect when everyone sees you off carousing with Jimmy Scott again?"

247

"I have my reasons for seeing him again, but I can't share them right now," Lydia mumbled.

"What on earth are you doing with him? And what happened with Aaron?"

Ruthie shifted uncomfortably in her seat as she poured tea into their glasses. "I'm really worried about this whole situation with you and Jimmy Scott. I don't trust him. Seeing you with him again... it's causing quite a stir in the community."

Lydia's jaw tightened, her fingers tracing the rim of her glass. "I know, and it's surely not helping my sales and customers issue."

"I'd think not!" Ruthie declared. "If you ever hoped to convince the bishop to lighten up some, your involvement with an *Englisher* again isn't going to help."

"I know!" Lydia exclaimed, "You don't need to remind me. I already know I'm burning bridges all over town that I might be unable to rebuild when the time is right."

With uncertainty hovering in the air, they settled down to enjoy their meal when suddenly, a thundering crash echoed from inside the bookshop. Their hearts pounded in unison as they exchanged alarmed glances, instinctively knowing that something was terribly wrong.

Without hesitating, Lydia sprang to her feet and instructed Ruthie. "Go out the back gate and call the police."

"Lydia, what in the world..." Ruthie's voice trembled with fear as she trailed off.

But Lydia's attention was already elsewhere as she headed back into the cellar. As her eyes adjusted to the darkness, she saw a series of bookshelves tipped over, strewing old books across the floor. In the chaos, she caught sight of a shadowy figure darting toward her, and all of a sudden, everything went dark as something was thrown over her head, and she was dragged into the damp passageway.

Panic surged through Lydia as she fought against the unseen assailant, her instincts screaming to break free. But the grip around her waist tightened, cutting off her cries for help as she was dragged further into the dark.

The musty air mixed with a familiar scent and the stench of her own fear as she struggled against her captor. Desperation clawed at her chest, looking for any means to escape as she was thrown into a room and left alone. When she fell to the floor, the door locked behind her, and she crawled on her hands and knees until her head hit the wall. Removing the covering from her head revealed nothing but a darkened room.

With each passing moment, Lydia's terror mounted, the sense of helplessness threatened to overwhelm her, but deep inside, a flicker of hope burned with the knowledge that Ruthie was summoning help.

CHAPTER 16

R uthie sprinted from the patio through the back gate and around to the front of the buildings along Main Street. She knew she needed to get help and fast. Terror gripped her at leaving Lydia alone.

Meanwhile, Aaron moved anxiously toward the bookshop, determined to talk some sense into Lydia. When he saw Ruthie running his way, her face pale with fear, he rushed to meet her, his heart already beating with dread.

"Ruthie, what is it? Where's Lydia?"

Breathless and wide-eyed, Ruthie sputtered, "Some... ...something crashed in the cellar, and she went inside... she... she made me go for help." She grabbed Aaron's arm. "I heard her scream as I was running away..."

Aaron's blood began to boil, and he was already running to the shop when she hollered..., "The door is locked; you'll need to go through the cellar!"

251

"Call Detective Powers!" Aaron bellowed as his mind raced, struggling to process the gravity of the situation.

As he approached the entrance, he heard Yankee barking and followed the dog's violent wails. With each step closer, his senses sharpened, and his every instinct was on finding Lydia. Searching frantically for a flashlight, he made his way to the spot where he and Lydia had discovered the entrance to the secret passage to the underground railroad.

As he reached the hidden bookshelf, Yankee's frantic barking pierced the silence, adding to his unease. He wasted no time opening the concealed entryway, allowing Yankee to take off in the dark.

***

In the distance, a scurry of muffled voices approached the darkened room. Lydia's heart sank like a stone in her chest as she listened to the heated exchange. She immediately recognized the voices—Ed Glick and Harvey.

Harvey's shouts bounced off the walls, each word laced with frustration. "What were you thinking? You've gone too far this time, and you've only made things worse!"

Ed's response was a deafening roar of angry words. "We need to get ahold of more books! How else were we supposed to..."

Harvey cut him off in a sound of fury. "You've ruined everything; my father was one thing, but Lydia...besides, I told you to stay away from my *schwester*, and that I was handling her."

His words were cut short by Yankee's bellowing bark. Their voices disappeared into the distance, and a cold knot formed in the back of Lydia's throat as she replayed their conversation in her head. The realization that her *bruder* may have had something to do with her father's death made her heave in despair. She thought they had devised a plan to settle Harvey's debts; why on earth would Ed still be after more books?

Yankee dashed into the tunnel, his loyal instincts driving him forward as Aaron followed close behind; the narrowing tunnels stretched in front of him were showered in darkness. But guided by Yankee's unwavering determination, he hollered Lydia's name along the way.

Lydia's voice echoed through the hidden chamber, announcing her location. With the end of the flashlight, Aaron busted the lock and flung open the door, rushing inside. Lydia's eyes filled with relief and gratitude as she collapsed into his arms.

At that moment, as they held each other tight, Aaron knew nothing else mattered but the safety of the woman he loved.

***

After Detective Lewis arrived at the bookshop, Lydia wasted no time recounting her terrifying encounter with Ed Glick and Harvey and explaining her sudden attention to Jimmy Scott to Aaron, her voice trembling as she described the whole ordeal.

The detective listened and exhaled when she finished. "I've been following some leads of my own, and this correlates to what I've discovered. I felt that Harvey might know about the tunnels, and I had already determined that Ed Glick was involved somehow."

Lydia sank into her father's easy chair, pulled her legs under her, and wrapped herself in a blanket to ward off a chill running down her back. "None of it makes sense," she whispered solemnly. "And why involve my father?"

Powers continued, "It seems Jimmy Scott's father's real

estate business has some deep ties to Markle and connections to the active black-market activity in Pittsburgh. They've been operating under the radar for years, targeting other Amish communities throughout western Pennsylvania. Do you think your brother might be involved with Markle?"

She shook her head. "I highly doubt it. All Harvey cares about is getting out of debt... that's where my father's books come in play." Lydia rested her face in her hands and moaned. "I just can't believe Harvey might have had something to do with *Datt's* murder." Lydia groaned. "There are just too many connections to my past, Ben Markle, and my father, not to mention I think you're right about it being some long planned out plan that goes back at least five years. But how does Harvey fit into all this?"

"I'm still trying to see if your brother is tied to the black market. All I know is we need to put a stop to it once and for all," he declared, his voice set in a determined tone. "First and foremost, Lydia, I need you to call Jimmy and convince him to return to the bookshop. We'll be here to ensure your safety."

Aaron had been quiet throughout the exchange, but with the detective's request, his face darkened with anger. "You're asking her to put herself in danger again? After everything she's been through. I don't like it one bit!"

Sitting beside her, Lydia placed a calming hand on Aaron's knee. "If it means getting to the bottom of my father's death and saving Main Street, how can I say no?"

The detective reassured him. "We'll only be a few steps away and positioned to rescue her if need be. Plus, we'll record every word in hopes he says something we can use to further our investigation."

"Isn't there another way?" Aaron pleaded.

Detective Powers turned his attention to Aaron. "I wish there was, but Lydia is our best chance."

Aaron nodded reluctantly, his features softening at Lydia's touch.

After she had calmed down and they had everything in place, Lydia scanned her phone to dial Jimmy, her hand shaking with nervous anticipation as she prepared to confront him. When he answered, she contrived distress, her voice quavering with fake emotion as she pleaded for his comfort and support.

Jimmy's response was anything but comforting and when he arrived at the bookshop, Lydia saw anger simmering beneath his surface. His eyes were dark; his jaw clenched as he walked toward her. She backed away instinctively, her pulse quickening with each step.

He relentlessly insisted that she sell the store and leave Willow Springs. As they spoke, Jimmy's frustration boiled over, his voice rising with each word until he practically shouted. He pinned Lydia against the counter, his towering frame hovering over her.

"Listen to me," he spat. "You're playing with fire by staying here, and you have no idea what you're up against if you don't do as I say."

Lydia twisted away. "I told you I'm not ready to sell. I have too much at stake right now to leave it all behind."

Jimmy grabbed her arm and rammed her into a nearby bookshelf. "You're just like your old man. Stubborn to the point of stupidity!"

The mention of her father sent warning bells ringing in Lydia's mind. How did Jimmy know her father, and what was the connection?

As she pressed for answers, Jimmy's façade began to change into an evil plot of revenge. Moving his hand to her throat, his words dripped like venom as he revealed the extent of his involvement with her father's death.

His admission hit Lydia like a brick, leaving her reeling with shock and disbelief. Her father had been using the picture of their baby to blackmail Jimmy, leveraging his reputation to keep his family from pressuring the Main Street merchants. And with Jimmy consumed by rage, he had taken matters into his own hands by quieting her father once and for all.

As Jimmy's words seethed in her ear, she felt a wave of revulsion washed over her. The man she once knew was gone, replaced with a monster fueled by hatred and vengeance. And she was his next target.

Before he tightened his fingers around her neck, she mumbled, "I'm not afraid of you."

He squeezed and moved his face so close to her face that his hot breath burned her cheek. "I should have done this a long time ago. You were nothing to me but a pawn to earn my father's respect."

With a surge of strength, Lydia drove a knee into him, causing him to double over in pain. She broke free, her heart pounding with adrenaline as she darted toward the door.

Jimmy cursed, lunging after her, his fingers brushing against her clothing as she narrowly escaped his grasp. Just as she reached the doorway, Aaron and Detective Powers tackled him to the ground. Their struggle crammed the room as Lydia stumbled out into the open air.

Grasping for breath, she hoped their ordeal was finally over until she realized with a sinking feeling that Aaron had just witnessed the darkest secret she'd kept hidden for years—the truth of why she ran away. The burden of facing him left her seizing in a wave of profound misery.

As Detective Powers handcuffed Jimmy, Lydia stood tall, refusing to allow him the satisfaction of seeing that he had rattled her. She met his stare despite the fear that gnawed her insides.

Jimmy spat venomous words at her and the others. "You think this is over? I'm just a small fish in a big pond. Bigger forces are at play here, and they won't stop until they get what they want."

The detective tightened his grip and pulled Jimmy away from Lydia, but she refused to give in to Jimmy's intimidation. "Like I said, I'm not afraid of you or your threats. Whatever forces are working here might have just met their match when taking over Willow Springs."

Jimmy spat on the floor, his eyes flashing with malice. "Yeah, right! You're naïve if you think a bunch of Amish are going to stop this." The detective drove him toward the door, but he continued to spit vile words at them. "You'll see this is far from over."

As the detective led Jimmy away, Lydia allowed herself to lean on Aaron as he pulled her close to his side. Aaron's presence was a reassuring glimmer of hope amid the chaos. But the truth remained the same—she had to face the consequences of her choices.

CHAPTER 17

Tears streamed down Lydia's cheeks as she found a glimmer of comfort in her father's worn easy chair. Mingling memories of her father's love and the weight of her past mistakes crushed her soul. She clasped her hands together tightly as if finding solace in the warmth of her own touch.

"Oh, *Datt*," she whispered, her voice trembling with sorrow. "I'm sorry... for everything."

Her heart ached with the weight of her confession as she replayed the choices she had made in her mind, each a painful reminder of the paths not taken, and the lives forever changed.

"Oh, *Gott,* forgive me," she whispered, her words choked with emotion. "I should have never let go of my child. I should have come home to seek your guidance and love instead of relying on my own understanding. But I was so lost, so scared... I didn't know what to do, and I should have gone to you first."

The thought of her lost child pierced her heart like a dagger, filling her with unmoving grief. She wished she could turn back time, undo the decisions, and step into Aaron's arms instead of Jimmy's. Go back and do things differently that had led her down this path and rewrite her story.

"How will I ever make amends for the pain I've caused, for the lives I've shattered?" she cried.

In the quiet of her small apartment, she yearned for the comfort of her father's company, for the reassurance that he would always love her, no matter what.

She sighed and picked up his journal. The pages were now tear-stained with frayed edges from her repeatedly reading his entries. Her father had poured out his love for her on the yellowed sheets. It was all she had left of him now, and she sobbed as she read his heartfelt pleas for her to come home.

She picked up her Bible and rested it on her knees as she bowed her head in prayer. She sought hope, believing that her heavenly father's love would never falter, and His grace would eventually lead her to redemption.

***

A warm summer breeze blew through as Lydia and Aaron

sat together at the small wrought iron table on the patio. Aaron lit the small oil lamp in the center of the table. The light danced between them as the tranquil sounds of crickets and a distant birdsong sang a melody around them.

Taking a moment to gather her thoughts, Lydia sought Aaron's eyes, hoping they revealed a deep understanding of what she was about to explain.

"Aaron," she began, her voice soft and lined with emotion. "I know you already know why I had to leave Willow Springs, but I want to explain it."

His look softened with understanding, his eyes reflecting the warmth of the late summer evening as he listened. With the flickering light between them, Aaron squeezed her hand. "You can tell me anything, Lydi," his voice a soothing comfort against the backdrop of the starlit sky.

It had been months since he had called her Lydi, and her heart melted in the palm of his hand. She took a deep breath and revealed the truth she'd kept hidden for years. "I... I should have come home," she moaned, "I shouldn't have given her away, and I'll never forgive myself for that."

Aaron nodded with empathy and support. "I've known for some time," he admitted quietly. "But I'm glad you're finally sharing it with me."

Tears welled up in Lydia's eyes as he leaned in and rested his cheek on hers. His dark beard tickled her cheek, and his clean, woodsy scent satisfied her nose. The burden of her choices seemed to melt away with his closeness. His understanding and comforting touch erased her fears, reminding her of the unwavering support she found in him.

Aaron's breath moved against her ear as he whispered, "This doesn't change how I feel about you. I've always sensed that this was why you left Willow Springs. I'd never hold it against you or let it be a reason not to work toward a future together."

Lydia caught a sob from releasing as she absorbed Aaron's words, feeling the warmth of his acceptance wash over her like a healing balm. But even amid his tender embrace, she couldn't shake the feeling that her past would come back, haunt them, and jeopardize his standing in the Old Order church.

"What about the church?" she asked, her voice trembling. "If they find out… you could be asked to choose between your church membership and me. The bishop won't look fondly on your relationship with me, notably with what I want to accomplish with the bookshop."

"If that's the case," he said firmly, "then I'll leave the Old Order and seek membership at the New Order Fellowship. But no matter what, I'll stand by your side."

"I'm so sorry for keeping this from you. I was afraid…"

But before she could continue, Aaron gently reached out and placed a finger on her lips, his eyes still overflowing with love.

"Lydi," he said softly, "our faith teaches us compassion and understanding. None of us are perfect, and we all have burdens to bear, but what matters most is that we face them together, with love and forgiveness."

Trying to control the raging sobs that were now flowing freely, she reached up, took his face in her hands, and gently kissed his lips through the tears.

They sat together for the next few minutes, hands intertwined, envisioning a future sealed with hope and promise.

Lydia's heart swelled with love for the man beside her; his unwavering devotion charged her with a love she had never experienced. As they gazed into each other's eyes, the shadows of the past began to dissipate, replaced by the glow of their renewed commitment to one another.

When a twinge of worry entered Lydia's mind, she inserted,

"I'm not sure God will ever forgive me for what I've done."

Aaron wrapped his strong hands around both of hers, rested his forehead on hers, and tenderly reminded her of *Gott's* love. "Our *Gott* is bigger than that, and He sees deep into our souls and knows every trial and tribulation we face."

Aaron's strong faith and resolve made Lydia shudder in thankfulness, but she still continued to doubt. "How can I ever be worthy of His love?"

Aaron lovingly reached up and wiped away her tears. "My dear Lydi, *Gott's* love knows no bounds. He sees beyond our faults and failures and embraces us with open arms. All we need is to trust in that."

Lydia couldn't speak, and all she could do was lean further into his embrace, letting her tears cover his shoulder. After all, she'd been through, *Gott* provided her a man who was a man of *Gott* through and through.

Before she could respond, cheerful chatter reached their ears, accompanied by the pitter-patter of tiny feet coming up the back sidewalk to the patio, followed by Aaron's mother.

"Lydia!" Mattie exclaimed, rushing forward and enveloping her with a tight hug. "I've missed you so much! Look what we found at the Thrift Store." Mattie Rose held out a stack of used books. Lydia couldn't help but laugh at her boundless enthusiasm. "Five books? You're becoming quite a little bookworm, aren't you?"

Mattie Rose nodded eagerly. "Like you, *jah.*"

As the little girl rattled on about each book, Lydia exchanged a loving glance with Aaron. It was clear that Mattie Rose's love for books had only grown in Lydia's presence, and she couldn't help but find joy in her excitement.

"I might have underestimated her love for reading," Aaron whispered with a hint of amusement in his voice.

Lydia chuckled softly, leaning in to kiss the little girl's forehead. "You know I need someone to help me with the bookshop."

With Mattie's infectious laughter filling the night air, Lydia felt a new wave of happiness. While no other child could ever take the place of her own daughter, the good Lord had provided a little girl to love and nurture in her place.

After seeing off Aaron's mother, Lydia offered popcorn, moving their visit upstairs.

With Mattie Rose busy exploring her thrift store find, Aaron sat at the counter while Lydia prepared a snack.

Aaron commented on Detective Powers' earlier visit as they

waited for the popcorn to finish. "They seemed to have enough evidence to put together a case about Scott Properties and Markle Media's involvement in the black market." He paused long enough to pour them all a drink and continued. "What will you do about Harvey's involvement in stealing your father's books?"

"Nothing," she said confidently. "I gladly handed them over to him to sell so he can settle his debt."

"And Ed Glick? What about him?"

"Now, I wouldn't mind putting that one away, but Lewis is convinced he has enough other stuff on him to take him off the streets for a good long time."

They allowed a comfortable silence to move between them over the sound of corn popping. "I want to approach the bishop about finding ways to make the bookshop a safe and welcoming place for everyone in the community, including the Amish children and their families," Lydia declared.

Aaron's eyebrows shot up in surprise, but they remained silent, waiting for her to continue.

"I've put a lot of thought into this. And even though the bishop's gut reaction was to ban my business, I want to explain my reasoning behind updating the store to attract more customers." She stopped long enough to pour popcorn into a small bowl and carry it to Mattie Rose, who was sprawled out on the floor in the other room.

When Lydia returned, she continued as Aaron filled his hand from the bowl. "I believe that by including things like the Internet Café' and other activities, I can create an environment that they feel safe in, keeping them off the street."

Aaron listened intently, nodding in understanding as Lydia laid out her plan.

"I want to work with those Amish teenagers who may be on the fence about staying Amish. If I can build a trusting relationship with them and be honest about my past, I may be able to convince them that the world isn't all it promises," she continued. "But to do that, I must find ways to entice them into the bookshop. I hope the bishop isn't so blind he doesn't realize they're curious. I'm hoping he'll agree to lift the ban on the bookshop so I can be a positive example in their lives. Someone they can go to. Someone they can trust to tell them the truth of the *Englisch* way of life."

Aaron squeezed her hand as she reached into the popcorn bowl, his eyes reflecting his admiration for her compassion for the young of their community. "I think that's a wonderful idea," he said softly. "And I'll support you every step of the way."

Suddenly, she knew her plan was coming together, and with Aaron's support, there was no doubt she'd be able to convince the community of her true intentions.

EPILOGUE
Christmas six months later…

The gentle dance of snowflakes painted the air outside the bookshop, swirling like feathers caught in a breeze. With a soft click, Lydia locked the door and flipped the sign to 'Closed' before turning down the lights and heading back upstairs.

For the past eight hours, her mind had been consumed with thoughts of the upcoming Christmas Tree Lighting Ceremony. Tonight was a special occasion for the entire Willow Springs community that everyone eagerly anticipated for weeks.

The evening promised a heartwarming blend of caroling and goodwill, supporting a worthy cause for the Willow Springs Orphanage. Making it even more special was Lydia's involvement in making sure the fourteen orphans had a Christmas they would remember for years to come. Lydia was especially looking forward to attending it with Aaron and

Mattie Rose.

Pausing for a moment, Lydia adjusted the red bow she had fastened to Yankee's leather collar, ensuring it sat just right. With a gentle pat, she reached for a treat from the jar on the counter and offered it to her loyal companion. As he happily nibbled on the biscuit, she bent down, wrapping her arms around his neck in a warm embrace.

"I know, buddy," she murmured softly. "You're not exactly happy about wearing this but think of how the children will love seeing you in it. You'll be the hit of the event, for sure and certain." Adjusting the bow again, she said, "I promise I'll take it off as soon as we get home."

As she finally shut off the last of the lights in the shop, she made her way upstairs to get ready for the evening. Aaron was never late, and she didn't want to keep him waiting.

It had been six months since she'd returned to Willow Springs, and Aaron along with Mattie Rose, played a huge part in her decision to rejoin the Amish community. She couldn't deny the deep love she felt for both of them; they had become her reason for embracing each new day.

Without Aaron's steadfast love and Mattie Rose's infectious laugh, she may have abandoned her father's cherished bookshop and returned to the bustling streets of Pittsburgh. But their love had shown her a different path, one saturated with the warmth and security of her Amish roots. It was a life she now cherished; one she couldn't imagine leaving behind.

Dressed in a new forest green dress, Lydia pinned it in place and put on a fresh white apron before adjusting her *kapp* securely. A hint of lavender oil on her wrists added a touch of calm to her excitement.

It was her first Christmas since returning, and she could barely contain her joy in the mere simplicity of it all. Drawing back the blue pleated curtain of her upstairs apartment window, Lydia looked eagerly down onto Main Street, searching for any sign of Aaron's buggy and saw the people already gathering in the park across the street.

As Lydia waited for Aaron to arrive, her heart fluttered with anticipation, her thoughts drifting back to his sweet marriage proposal just a week earlier...

It had been a late evening sleigh ride, the snowy landscape around them covered in its own wintery magic. Aaron had guided the sleigh to the side of the road, and as the snow fell gently around them like a soft blanket, he reached for both of her hands, holding them to his chest.

"I promise to love you with all that I am," he said, his voice soaked in tenderness. "Will you be my fraa?"

Lydia had felt her heart fill with his love as he kissed the snowflakes from her lips, and with a soft breath, she had whispered, "Jah."

Summoning Yankee to join her downstairs, she secured his lead as soon as they reached the door. "Let's wait outside for Aaron," she suggested, knowing the fresh air would be invigorating for both her and the eager dog.

As she balanced her keys and Yankee's lead, Lydia was caught off guard by the soft jingle of sleigh bells. The beautiful sound stopped behind her as she locked the door, and when she turned towards the street, she was met with the heartwarming sight of Aaron and Mattie Rose; their faces lit up with joy.

"Lydia, *Datt* brought the sleigh." Mattie Rose chimed excitedly.

It was hard not to be touched by Mattie Rose's cheerfulness, and Lydia found herself at a loss for words as she stood next to the sleigh. Mattie Rose's excitement bubbled over; her six-year-old chatter was nonstop as if she had indulged in one too many candy canes.

Lydia giggled, helping her down from the sleigh. "I remember how exciting Christmas was when I was a child. My *datt* made it special." Laughter bubbled between them as Aaron secured the horses to a hitching post.

As Mattie Rose held her head high, catching snowflakes on her tongue, Lydia looped her arm through Aaron's and lightly squeezed. "Everything is just perfect for my first Christmas back home." There was a sweetness beyond words in the air, and the effect of the season was enchanting. Aaron whispered, "Merry Christmas."

In that magical moment, Lydia felt a sense of peace and contentment, believing life couldn't get any better. As they approached the park, children's carolers stood at the entrance, welcoming people closer to the tree.

They all stood in awe of the glorious sights and sounds, and Aaron whispered in Lydia's ear. "I believe she's speechless enough to be quiet for a few minutes." They both giggled as Aaron tipped his hat to a couple they passed.

After a round of hot chocolate, the sweet acapella voices of the choir faded, and the mayor took the podium. "Thank you for all coming tonight. What a wonderful turnout for our annual event." He rested, allowing the applause to cease. "I'm delighted to see so many of our Amish neighbors here tonight. It warms my heart to see us all come together for the better of Willow Springs after the year we had." He looked around the crowd before continuing. "And we can thank one woman in particular for all her hard work in preserving Main Street and for generously volunteering to make this Christmas special for the orphans of Willow Springs. Lydia Troyer, will you please join me on the stage?"

Lydia's heart skipped a beat as she exchanged a quick glance with Aaron and handed off Yankee. Stepping forward to join the mayor at the podium, she excitedly shivered. With a nod from the mayor, the towering blue spruce burst into brilliant lights, making a joyful noise from the crowd. As the excitement settled, the mayor passed the microphone to Lydia, and she trod forward to address the gathering. Turning to the orphans assembled on the stage, she gave them a warm smile before addressing the audience.

"There's no greater gift we can offer these children than the warmth of a loving home, even if it's for a short time during the Christmas season," Lydia declared. She turned toward the children's eager faces, and her eyes settled on the small girl at the end of the row. For some reason, she looked familiar, and it took her a moment to gather her thoughts before continuing, "And today, we have something truly special in store for you…"

Her eyes turned back to the little brown-haired girl when she remembered… it was the girl from the park, and her heart swelled with emotion. "We're offering the gift of family this Christmas. Some of us have opened our hearts and homes to you. You'll experience the joy of the holidays surrounded by love and warmth."

Through the chorus of excited cheers from the children, Lydia began calling out each child's name, pairing them with their host family.

As the last child, Julia Jenkins, stood alone on the stage, Lydia called out her name. The shy brown-haired girl stepped forward, her face lighting up with a shy smile of recognition.

"Julia," Lydia said warmly, kneeling to meet her at eye level. "You'll be spending Christmas with me and my family." Julia leaned in close, her voice barely above a whisper. "I've been praying you would pick me."

Lydia's heart swelled with emotion at the sincerity of the girl's words. She wrapped her arms around her in a tight embrace, whispering back, "Your prayers have been answered."

***

Christmas morning at Lydia's apartment was full of surprises. Aaron had allowed Mattie Rose to spend the night, allowing the two fast friends to wake up together. Aaron arrived before dawn carrying a few presents, and Lydia had filled stockings with treats and placed them at their places at the table.

With morning rising above the horizon, she lit candles she had positioned in the pine boughs Aaron had delivered the day before.

Cinnamon and vanilla wafted through the air in the apartment as the rolls she made the night before baked and just as she took them from the oven, Aaron took both of her hands in his own, turning her to face him. Bringing her knuckles to his lips and looking tenderly into her eyes, he asked, "Before the girls get up, there's something I'd like to ask you."

Lydia's heart skipped a beat as she waited on his every word.

"You know this apartment isn't big enough for a family."

Lydia giggled. "Well, right now I don't have a family so it's plenty big enough for me."

Aaron gave her a stern but gentle nudge. "You're right, but I'm praying that won't be the case for long."

Lydia smiled a knowing grin and ask, "And?"

Aaron snickered. "You surely aren't making this easy on a guy."

"I'm not the one with the question," she muttered back amusingly.

"Come now, I've already asked you to be my *fraa*, but you've failed to tell me when I can expect that to happen."

Lydia stood on her tiptoes to reach his ear, letting his whiskers tickle her cheek. "Is next month too soon?"

Aaron engulfed her in a hug and whispered back, "It's not soon enough for me, but it will have to do."

Before they had a chance to finish their conversation, Mattie Rose and Julia emerged from the bedroom, their faces alight with anticipation. Mattie Rose snuggled on her father's lap, while Julia settled onto Lydia's, clutching a quilt close to her chest.

Lydia's breath caught in her throat as she touched the fabric, her fingers trembling with emotion.

"That's a beautiful quilt. Where did you get it?" she asked, her voice barely above a whisper.

Julia hugged the quilt tightly. "Mommy said I was wrapped in it when God gave me to her." Julia hesitated for a few seconds and snuggled into Lydia's embrace more tightly before adding, "I tried to give it to Mommy before she went to live with Jesus, but she said God was going to use it to help me find my new mommy."

Lydia could hardly breathe as she took in the sight of the quilt she had lovingly used to wrap her daughter in before giving her away.

"Is it Christmas now?" Julia inquired; her eyes wide with wonder.

"It is indeed. Would you like to open your present?" Lydia offered gently.

But Julia shook her head, her brown eyes shimmering with emotion. "I don't need to open it. I have it right here." With that, she wrapped her arms around Lydia, nestling into her chest. "You are my Christmas."

As Lydia looked across the room and met Aaron's eyes, she saw the same understanding reflected in his eyes. They shared a silent moment of realization, their revelation settling upon them like a warm embrace. Julia was more than just an orphan;

she was Lydia's long-lost child, miraculously reunited with her mother on Christmas.

With tears streaming down her face, Lydia wrapped her arms around her daughter, holding her close as if she never wanted to let go. At that moment, she knew that her return to Willow Springs was all in *Gott's* ultimate plan. And as she looked into Julia's eyes, she saw the same spark of recognition, the same unspoken bond that connected them forever.

Together, Lydia and Aaron marveled at the wonder of it all, the joy and the sorrow, the pain and the healing that brought them all together as a family. And as they held each other close, they knew this Christmas would be a celebration like no other, a true blessing and a testament to the power of love, forgiveness, and the enduring hope of miracles.

***

Read the next book in the Willow Springs Amish Mystery Romance series. ***The Amish Baker Caper.***

When Ruthie Mast's prized recipe box disappears, so does the peace in Willow Springs. Dive into ***The Amish Baker Caper*** as the bold and bossy Ruthie and the quirky Isaiah King team up to untangle a web of thefts, unsettling their tranquil Amish community.

The Amish

Baker Caper

A WILLOW SPRINGS
AMISH MYSTERY ROMANCE

Book 2

Tracy Fredrychowski

Tracy Fredrychowski

PROLOGUE

Thefts Rattle Amish Community

by Jonas Butler – The Hemlock Star

Residents of Willow Springs have been left shaken by a recent string of thefts plaguing their peaceful community. The crimes, which began last week, have targeted several prominent businesses as well as members of the New Order Fellowship Church, leaving residents scrambling for answers.

The incidents, including the disappearance of valuable items, have affixed a sense of discord to the once-tranquil Amish community. Concerns for safety and security have encouraged church leaders to warn their members to take extra precautions to protect their belongings.

Local baker Ruthie Mast was among the first to discover her treasured recipe box missing. "I can't understand why anyone would take such a personal item. It holds no monetary value," Mast remarked. "Some of the recipes are over one hundred years old, handed down to me by my mother and grandmother."

Detective Powers from the Willow Springs Police Department has launched an investigation into the crimes but has yet to identify any suspects. "We are treating this series of crimes with the utmost seriousness," stated Powers. "Our priority is to ensure the safety and security of all residents throughout Willow Springs."

The sudden wave of strange events has prompted speculation within the community, with some members expressing concern about the potential outsider targeting the Amish. Others fear that the crimes may be the work of someone within their own midst, leading to strained relations among neighbors.

In the wake of the thefts, residents are urged to remain vigilant and report any suspicious activity to authorities. Despite the challenges facing the community, there is hope that the perpetrators will be brought to justice and that peace will once again be restored to Willow Springs.

Tracy Fredrychowski

CHAPTER 1

April had arrived in Northwestern Pennsylvania, breathing new life into Willow Springs. Along Main Street, the businesses stirred to activity, their doors swinging open to welcome the new day. The towering maple trees that lined the cobblestone street swayed in a gentle breeze, their branches beginning to embrace the subtle transition of spring.

Ruthie Mast stood behind the counter of her beloved bakery, The Amish Baker, kneading the dough with practiced hands as the smell of fresh bread occupied the air. The morning sun streamed through the windows, highlighting her collection of mismatched tables and chairs and the full case of pastries waiting to be consumed.

Despite the inviting welcome to a new day, Ruthie couldn't shake the melancholy that lingered within her after learning about another of her friends' impending marriages. As she worked, her mind wandered to the ache of loneliness that gnawed at her heart. In a community as small as Willow Springs, eligible suitors were few and far between, and she had scared away the ones that were left with her abrupt personality. She couldn't help but feel left behind as she watched her friends pair off and start families.

Lost in her thoughts, Ruthie barely saw the familiar figure of her best friend, Lydia Troyer, owner of the Book Cellar, standing at the counter. Her gentle smile and chestnut hair tucked tightly under her pressed white *kapp* greeted her with a warm hello. "Morning, Ruthie." Lydia lifted her nose and moaned, "It smells wonderful in here."

Ruthie managed a small smile in return, grateful for the distraction her friend provided. "Good morning. What brings you by this morning?"

Lydia approached the bakery case. "I couldn't help myself; the smells lingering up and down the street made my stomach growl."

Ruthie let out a small sigh, and Lydia moved to the counter with a troubled statement. "You seem a bit down this morning. Is everything alright?"

Ruthie covered the dough to rise, wiped her hands on a towel, and leaned against the butcher block worktable. "Oh,

Lydia, it's just… I don't think I'll ever find anyone to share life with." She exhaled and resumed, "I hate feeling like this, but I must admit I'm a little jealous of you and Annie. You have Aaron, and now Annie's getting married too. When will it be my turn?"

Lydia moved to the coffee station and poured them a fresh cup and invited her to join her at a table under the front window.

"I understand, Ruthie. I can only imagine how hard it is to stand back and watch others find love while you're still searching for your own." Lydia reached out and patted the back of her hand. "Love has a way of finding you in the most inconspicuous circumstances."

Ruthie nodded. "But there is no one in Willow Springs who catches my eye, no eligible members in our community I'd even consider for a husband."

Lydia snickered. "Could it be your expectations are too high?"

"Oh, believe me, I've considered accepting any attraction that might come my way, but I'm twenty-seven and probably should be considering membership into the Good Apple Girls Club instead."

"Now stop, Ruthie. You're hardly ready for a permanent

membership into the single girl's club."

Lydia crossed her legs and leaned her chin into the palm of her hand. "What about Jacob Kauffman? He's a hardworking farmer with a good heart."

Ruthie scoffed, her frustration bubbling to the surface. "Jacob? Please. He's as dull as dishwater. I need someone with more to offer than just cows and corn."

Lydia frowned at her dismissive tone. "Well, what about Samuel Glick? He's a skilled carpenter and could provide you with a good home and security."

Ruthie rolled his eyes, shaking her head in disbelief. "Samuel? He's too preoccupied with his work to even notice a woman. I need someone who can give me their undivided attention."

As Ruthie and Lydia exchanged their thoughts, a sudden commotion drew their attention to the street outside. Startled, they exchanged worrisome glances before rushing outside to investigate.

The once peaceful morning buzzed with tension as shouts burst through the air. A group of masked individuals sprinted past them down Main Street, their faces obscured by dark fabric. Behind them, the security guard from the bank pursued, the glint of his badge catching the sunlight.

Fear gripped Ruthie as she observed the scene unfold. "Lydia, what's happening?"

Lydia shook her head, her voice barely above a whisper. "I don't know, but we should stay back. That's the bank guard. I'm almost certain of it." Looking down toward the bank, nothing seemed amiss. "There's something not right about this."

They stood frozen; their attention drawn to the chaos unfolding in the street when a sudden loud crash echoed from inside the bakery. Their heads whipped around in unison; their eyes wide in alarm.

"What was that?" Lydia exclaimed, her voice trembling in fear.

Ruthie's heart hammered in her chest as she exchanged a worried glance with Lydia. Without hesitation, they rushed back inside, their senses on high alert. Dread gnawed at Ruthie's stomach as she feared what they might find.

As they crossed the threshold, Ruthie's worst fears were confirmed. The once tidy bake shop lay in shambles. The glass case had been smashed, and the bakery rack turned over, spilling fresh baked goods all over the floor. But the most devastating sight was the empty space where Ruthie's treasured recipe box should have been.

***

Read the next book in the Willow Springs Amish Mystery Romance series. *The Amish Baker Caper.*

When Ruthie Mast's prized recipe box disappears, so does the peace in Willow Springs. Dive into *The Amish Baker Caper* as the bold and bossy Ruthie and the quirky Isaiah King team up to untangle a web of thefts, unsettling their tranquil Amish community.

WHAT DID YOU THINK?

First of all, thank you for purchasing *The Amish Book Cellar – A Willow Springs Mystery Romance*. I hope you will enjoy all the books in this series.

You could have picked any number of books to read, but you chose this book, and for that, I am incredibly grateful. I hope it added value and quality to your everyday life. If so, it would be nice to share this book with your friends and family on social media.

If you enjoyed this book and found some benefit in reading it, I'd like to hear from you and hope that you could take some time to post a review on Amazon. Your feedback and support will help me improve my writing craft for future projects.

If you loved visiting Willow Springs, I invite you to sign up for my private email list, where you'll get to explore more of the characters of this Amish Community.

Sign up at https://dl.bookfunnel.com/v9wmnj7kve and download the novella that starts this series, *The Amish Women of Lawrence County*.

GLOSSARY
Pennsylvania Dutch "Deutsch" Words

Ausbund. Amish songbook.

bruder. B, but she didn't utter dad.

denki. Thank You.

doddi. Grandfather.

doddi house. A small house next to the main house.

g'may. Community

goot meiya. Good morning.

jah. Yes.

kapp. Covering or prayer cap.

kinner. Children.

mamm. Mother or mom.

mommi. Grandmother.

nee. No.

Ordnung. Order or set of rules the Amish follow.

rumshpringa. Running around period.

schwester. Sister.

singeon. Singing/youth gathering.

The Amish are a religious group typically referred to as Pennsylvania Dutch, Pennsylvania Germans, or Pennsylvania Deutsch. They are descendants of early German immigrants to Pennsylvania and their beliefs center around living a conservative lifestyle. They arrived between the late 1600s and the early 1800s to escape religious persecutions in Europe. They first settled in Pennsylvania with the promise of religious freedom by William Penn. Most Pennsylvania Dutch still speak a variation of their original German language as well as English.

Tracy Fredrychowski

ABOUT THE AUTHOR

Tracy Fredrychowski's life closely mirrors the gentle, simple stories she crafts in her writing. With a passion for the simpler side of life, Tracy regularly shares tips on her website and blog at tracyfredrychowski.com

In northwestern Pennsylvania, Tracy grew up steeping in the virtues of country living. A pivotal moment in her life was the tragic murder of a young Amish woman in her community. This event profoundly influenced her, compelling her to dedicate her writing to the peaceful lives of the Amish people. Tracy aims to inspire her readers through her stories to embrace a life centered around faith, family, and community.

For those intrigued by the Amish way of life, Tracy extends an invitation to connect with her on Facebook. On her page and group, she shares captivating Amish photography by her friend Jim Fisher and recipes, short stories, and glimpses into her cherished Amish community nestled deep in the heart of northwestern Pennsylvania's Amish County.

Facebook.com/tracyfredrychowskiauthor/

Facebook.com/groups/tracyfredrychowski/

Printed in Great Britain
by Amazon

43336259R00179